HEARTS IN PERIL™

A Sinister Silence

Jan Fields

Annie's®
AnniesFiction.com

Books in the Hearts in Peril series

Buried Memories
In Too Deep
Christmas Conspiracy
A Deadly Game
Dangerous Prospects
A Sinister Silence
Bayou Cold Case
Fatal Artifacts
A Chilling Reunion
Remote Danger
Terror on the Trail
Safe Haven Stalker

... and more to come!

A Sinister Silence
Copyright © 2023, 2024 Annie's.

All rights reserved. No part of this publication may be reproduced, stored in a retrieval system, or transmitted in any form or by any means—electronic, mechanical, photocopying, recording or otherwise—without the prior written permission of the publisher. The only exception is brief quotations in printed reviews. For information address Annie's, 306 East Parr Road, Berne, Indiana 46711-1138.

The characters and events in this book are fictional, and any resemblance to actual persons or events is coincidental.

Library of Congress-in-Publication Data
A Sinister Silence / by Jan Fields
p. cm.
ISBN: 979-8-89253-203-7
I. Title
     2022947586

AnniesFiction.com
(800) 282-6643
Hearts in Peril™
Series Creator: Shari Lohner
Series Editor: Amy Woods

10 11 12 13 14 | Printed in China | 9 8 7 6 5 4 3 2

1

The Cornelius Institute in New York City was a hideously pricey private college, and no expense had been spared in making it ooze prestige. The marble floor in the entry of the psychology building was proof enough of that. Who bothered with marble in a building filled mostly with classrooms and cramped professor offices?

Dr. Virginia Bryce's heels rang on the stone floor as she kept up a brisk pace through the lobby. She turned sharply down the right-hand wing as soon as the opportunity arose. She kept her eyes focused directly ahead and her chin raised. She could project an image of stature and success every bit as well as the pretentious building around her. She was vaguely aware that the walls were lined with portraits of the school's famous alumni, hung mostly to convince visitors that graduates of the Cornelius Institute were guaranteed to go on to live wealthy and successful lives. Of course, they'd started out wealthy, which had played a large part in their ultimate success, but that wasn't what the college cared to promote.

Ginny loathed such excessive display, such a grand facade. She understood the psychology behind it, but that didn't mean she approved of anything to do with the college. The sole reason she was there at all was that the dean of the School of Psychology was Wilfred Baylor. Five years before, Wilfred's young son, Jonathan, had been kidnapped. The family had paid the ransom, and the boy was returned, but the experience had traumatized Jonathan into night terrors, bed-wetting, and bouts of destructive rage.

As Ginny already had a reputation for handling such cases in her practice, Wilfred and his wife had brought Jonathan to her. She could still remember the desperate worry on their faces and the dark smears under the child's eyes from lack of sleep. Ginny had taken on Jonathan's therapy for nearly a year, and the last time she'd seen him, the boy showed no sign of the horrors of his ordeal. He'd finally put them behind him.

During the child's therapy sessions, one thing stood out strongly to Ginny—Wilfred's fierce love for his son. The father hadn't cared about the family name or scandal or any of the things Ginny's richer clients tended to bring up before hiring her to heal a broken child. Wilfred had cared about nothing but Jonathan's healing.

That was what had swayed her into agreeing when Wilfred asked her to speak at the haughty school. Having second thoughts as she walked, Ginny considered her agreement a lapse in judgment and was annoyed with herself. She feared she might spend the hour talking to people who would rather pay attention to their phones than to anything she might have to say.

"Dr. Bryce?" Willow Reed sounded winded, and Ginny slowed down. Willow was ten years younger than Ginny but sometimes found it challenging to keep up with her boss's energetic pace. In all other ways, Willow was an excellent assistant. And Ginny rather admired the self-confidence reflected in Willow's sometimes unorthodox choices of hair color and clothing.

Willow had recited the list of things Ginny absolutely must accomplish. Each of the items should be done before Ginny left the city to retreat to the wilds of Pennsylvania and finish writing her second book. Though she recognized the importance of the tasks, she had stopped responding as Willow ticked off her list.

"I'm aware of all of those commitments," Ginny said when Willow stopped talking, probably to catch her breath. "I'll see to it that my schedule is free and clear before I leave."

"All right," Willow said. "But there are so many things. Are you sure leaving now is a good idea? People are going to end up mad at you."

"People are always mad at me."

"There's that, but I'll be the one answering angry phone calls while you're gone."

Ginny didn't snap at the young woman, nor remind Willow that answering phone calls was part of her job description. Though Ginny did not enjoy having her choices second-guessed, she also knew Willow was correct. It was not a good idea to disappear and leave so many things up in the air, but it was necessary.

She'd missed two deadlines on the book already, and her publisher grew increasingly impatient. Her agent wasn't much more forgiving. Ginny was smart enough to accept that she would never finish the book if she didn't get away from all her other demands and write. And if she was honest, she needed a break from other peoples' pain.

"I wouldn't go to a cabin in the woods if it weren't necessary," Ginny said stiffly. She'd hated the cabin in the Pennsylvania forest when it was her survivalist family's home, and she'd nearly had it destroyed when she inherited it a decade ago. But something had made her reconsider. Instead, she'd poured a lot of money into transforming the cabin, making it unrecognizable from the past, simply so she could walk through the door without fighting the urge to curl into a ball. It would never be the true haven of peace she wanted, but at least it was well away from the city.

"Fine," Willow said in resignation. "But I have one last thing. I made a packet of some of the mail you've gotten recently. There are a few letters from parents of past patients with updates on their children.

There are a few from people writing about your last book. And then there are the creepy ones. I thought you should see them so you can decide if you need to do something about any of them."

"Do something?" Ginny echoed as she headed down another corridor, which led to the small auditorium where she was scheduled to give her talk.

"There are some threats."

Ginny took care not to show her exasperation at the topic. "It's not surprising that I get hate mail. I've worked with the police, and I've gotten a lot of publicity. Hate mail happens. I don't need to read it. They'll get over it."

Willow halted in her tracks, though Ginny kept walking. "How can you be so nonchalant? What if one of these letters is related to whoever broke into your car?"

"It's a nice car," Ginny said, pivoting to face her assistant. "Thieves break into nice cars. It's not related."

"It could be. And if so, it could escalate until someone breaks into your apartment."

"That seems reasonable. While I'm out of town, will you stop by my apartment a few times? If you find signs of vandalism or robbery, call the police. And then hire a painter or order new furniture—whatever is needed. I'll take care of any invoices for it when I get back." With that, she moved on to the auditorium doors.

"All right." Willow sprinted to reach the doors first, opening one for Ginny. "You'll be great."

Ginny gave Willow a tight smile that she hoped conveyed some gratitude, then straightened her shoulders and walked in. The floors of the auditorium were carpeted. Judging from the softness under Ginny's feet, no expense had been spared there either. Students filled the seats, chatting with the other young people around them.

Heading up the center aisle, Ginny kept her eye on the stage where Wilfred Baylor stood at the center podium, clutching a piece of paper and squinting toward Ginny. She inclined her head slightly in response to his relieved expression and climbed the steps to the stage. When he met her at the top, she thrust out her hand to shake.

Ginny knew she often came across as standoffish and that it didn't exactly soften people's perception of her, but she didn't worry much about it. In truth, she'd never been particularly lighthearted. As a child, she'd found no amusement in the difficult life she'd lived. Sometimes it still felt as if she carried entirely too much weight, manifesting as tension in her neck and shoulders that left her aching some days.

For the last five years, she'd taken on fewer and fewer clients until she'd stopped seeing anyone at all. She'd hoped that would result in the weight lifting, but that hadn't happened. It didn't help that her colleagues often contacted her with pleas to consult on difficult cases. Over the years of her active practice, Ginny had developed a reputation for being a miracle worker with traumatized children, and she was acutely aware that a suffering child existed at the other end of every request she received. That suffering hurt her heart. But she couldn't live for other people all the time. Hadn't she given enough?

"I'm so glad you are here," Wilfred said warmly. "My students are eager to hear what you have to say."

Ginny hoped so but knew Wilfred might simply say that to offer support, so she kept her comments to herself. Instead, she said, "It's good to see you, Wilfred."

"And you, Ginny."

To Ginny's great surprise, the students stopped talking amongst themselves and focused on the stage as she walked to stand beside the podium. Wilfred introduced her. "We are honored today with a visit from Dr. Virginia Bryce, author of *Mending the Broken Child*.

She'll be speaking with us today about the myth of childhood resiliency."

Ginny took her spot at the podium to a healthy amount of applause. She surveyed the audience and found that every face she saw reflected interest in what she had to say. Her talk could be far better than she'd expected.

Ginny took a sip from the water glass provided, then began. "How often have we heard that children bounce back, that they get over pain even when it's from serious trauma, that they are resilient? This belief often leads to parents rejecting therapy for children who would benefit from it, expecting them to simply outgrow significant issues that negatively affect their well-being. The myth of the resilient child has allowed untreated childhood trauma to result in untold numbers of broken adults."

As she spoke, Ginny scanned the audience. She didn't focus on any one person, flitting from face to face so that no unexpected expression could throw her off her train of thought. She found that surveying the audience helped her gauge the general feeling of a room and make adjustments to her presentation if necessary. Confused frowns would clue her in that the audience needed more grounding in the subject. Bored expressions encouraged her to pick up the pace or throw in an entertaining anecdote.

It was as she scanned the attentive young faces that she spotted the one anomaly in the room, a man seated not far from the stage. He was older than most of the audience, about forty. Age alone wasn't that much of an outlier. The audience was sprinkled with older people, some even sporting gray hair. It wasn't unusual for professors to arrange their schedules so they could hear her speak, and many colleges welcomed the public at special guest lectures. But the man didn't strike her as a professor or a student, despite the intent expression on his handsome features.

The stranger's jeans, T-shirt, and battered leather jacket were too casual for a professor. The muscles his outfit did nothing to hide were impressive as well. He put time into that build. Ginny allowed her attention to slip to him again. Maybe a coach? Or a cop? That last thought made her groan inwardly. It wasn't impossible that an NYPD detective would show up, hoping to pull her into a case.

Her thoughts caused her eyes to linger on the man too long, and he noticed, offering her a dazzling grin. She jerked her attention away from him and forced herself not to look in his direction again. Whatever problem he represented, she'd deal with it later. If he proved to be a cop, he'd soon find out that she wasn't interested in helping. In fact, if she was quick, she may be able to get off the stage before he reached her.

A smile tugged at the corner of her mouth. She could be very quick indeed. After all, as a child, she'd had years of hard lessons in getting away from all the scary things in the world.

Shifting slightly in the seat to stretch his long legs, Joseph Macklin never took his eyes off Dr. Virginia Bryce. She was an excellent speaker, but he'd expected that. He'd read enough about her to know that Dr. Bryce appeared to be good at virtually anything she decided to do. He admired that about her. He respected determined people, and he watched her carefully as her eyes flicked over the audience frequently, alert and aware.

He had considered taking notes on her speech about childhood trauma in case she said anything that might help. So far, he hadn't picked up any info that would aid Benji. He already knew his nephew needed help and wanted to find him the best therapist to unlock whatever was going on inside the boy's head. His research said the best childhood trauma therapist in the country stood on the stage before him. Her colleagues described her as brilliant, but her assistant had rebuffed all his efforts to make an appointment with Dr. Bryce. She wasn't seeing patients, he'd been told—no exceptions.

But Mac, a nickname he'd picked up in high school that had never gone away, refused to take no for an answer. Not when it involved protecting his family. Protection was Mac's business, and he took it seriously. As the co-owner of a sought-after security firm that specialized in bodyguards and security systems, Mac knew his bread and butter lay in making people feel safe, but when it came to one six-year-old boy, he was failing completely. Benji's nightmares woke him screaming, which was the only time the boy made any sound at all.

As soon as the lecture ended, Mac sprang to his feet, fully expecting the psychologist to bolt. Before she'd arrived, the dean had warned the audience that Dr. Bryce would not be taking questions, nor would she stick around afterward. But Mac would do anything to get his nephew the help Benji so desperately needed.

Having done his homework on the Cornelius Institute, he knew the layout of the building perfectly. He'd already dismissed the idea of running for the stairs leading to the stage. The dean would slow him down. The situation called for something more direct. He was out the front door even as he heard voices calling to Dr. Bryce as she made her own dash for an exit on the other side of the stage.

Separate short corridors linked the two front exits to the main hall, so Mac raced to the main hall, then swerved toward the second short corridor, the one Dr. Bryce would use. He met her as she reached the end.

Moving with surprising quickness, the psychologist tried to step around him. Mac gave way, falling into step beside her. She walked fast, but she wasn't able to outpace his long-legged stride. "Dr. Bryce," he said. "My name is Joseph Macklin. I need your help."

Despite their near sprint down the hall, her response was not the slightest bit winded. "I no longer assist the police, Mr. Macklin."

"You can call me Mac."

"Not going to happen. As I said, I do not work with the police, so if you'll excuse me, there's somewhere I need to be."

"I'm not the police," Mac said. "I need your help for my nephew, Benji."

"I do not take private cases either."

"But you could. And my nephew needs you."

"I'm sorry."

"I won't give up, Dr. Bryce," he said. "Benji is too important."

She stopped so quickly that he passed her, then stumbled as he spun to face her. She was scowling at him. She reached into the pocket of her neat gray blazer and held out a card. "Call this number. My assistant will be happy to give you a list of competent therapists who can help your nephew."

Mac didn't even touch the card. "I learned a long time ago not to settle for 'competent' when 'excellent' is so much better. And in this case, I absolutely cannot compromise. My nephew is six years old. His parents died in a car accident. He was in the car. He hasn't spoken since. And he's suffering. I'm responsible for him, and I will do everything I can for my brother's son."

She didn't interrupt as he spoke, and he appreciated that and took hope from it, despite the fury in her eyes.

"I won't give up," he insisted. "A child's well-being is at stake."

Dr. Bryce crossed her arms over her chest and glared at him. It was an impressive glare, but Mac had learned to read people in his work too, and he sensed she was considering his request.

"How long ago was this accident?"

"Six weeks."

"Was your nephew injured?"

Mac shook his head. "He had a top-of-the-line car seat. My sister-in-law didn't fool around about safety where her family was concerned." A wave of sadness threatened to swamp him, but he pushed it down ruthlessly. "The doctors said Benji was probably sore, but if so, he never complains. He doesn't speak now. At all."

"How was he before the accident?" she asked. "What sort of personality?"

"Smart. Funny. Fearless." Mac felt sorrow spread through him again. "I barely recognize him now. He draws a lot." He pulled a folded paper from his jacket pocket and held it out.

She stared at it, as if considering whether to accept it, then took the paper and carefully unfolded it. She examined the drawing without a visible reaction. Mac knew the picture well. He'd seen it, and dozens almost identical to it, in the past weeks. The drawing was done in black crayon, the sole color Benji used anymore. It was the face of a howling monster with huge, round, blank eyes.

"They all show the same monster," Mac said. "Sometimes up close, sometimes farther away. You can see the monster has another eye growing out of its chest."

"It isn't uncommon for children of your nephew's age to personify their fears," she said, though her gaze stayed locked on the drawing.

"There's something else," Mac said. "Benji was the most extroverted kid you ever met. He'd start up a chat about his favorite dinosaur with strangers on the subway, and even the grumpiest would be won over by the time they reached their stop."

Dr. Bryce nodded in acknowledgment, still studying the drawing. "And now he doesn't talk."

"It's more than that. He doesn't want to be around people at all. When he's not drawing, he's standing at the windows of my apartment, staring out at the street. At first, I thought maybe he was searching for his parents, hoping they'd come home, but I don't think that's what's going on."

Finally the doctor raised her eyes to meet his. "What do you think is going on?"

"I think he is watching for someone, but not Derrick and Madison, because whoever he's expecting to see scares him. A lot. And I need to know what or whom it is. Because if this is someone real, I need to know so I can keep him safe. I need your help."

2

The tall man before her was clearly used to getting his own way, partially because of his size, though she had no doubt his rugged good looks also played a part. Knowing he expected her to fold made her want to refuse him all the more. He may have a history of people bending under his will, but she had plenty of her own will. "I believe I've made my position clear, Mr. Macklin."

"As have I," he said.

The two stared at one another in the hallway, and Ginny noticed that the big man's eyes weren't quite blue as she'd thought at first glance. They were gray, something she didn't think she'd seen before. She realized they were spending a ridiculous amount of time staring boldly into each other's eyes, and she began to feel silly.

She wanted to run suddenly, simply sprint down the hall and leave the man and his demands behind, but she doubted she could outrun his much-longer stride. She never doubted that if she tried to walk away, he'd follow and keep following. She folded her arms over her chest and frowned. At least the case didn't sound horrific. His nephew hadn't experienced the kind of horrors that would haunt her nightmares. From what she'd heard so far, Benji was the product of a healthy home and loving parents. His mutism was probably his way of dealing with having witnessed something so painful, while helpless to stop it.

"It isn't abnormal for a child who has lost his parents to watch for their return, even in a situation like this where Benji knows his parents are dead."

"I told you, that's not what he's watching for," the big man said, pointing at the paper Ginny still held. "He's scared, Doctor. He's scared of whatever this is."

And you're paranoid. But Ginny could hardly fault the man for that. Paranoia had been baked into her childhood. She had no doubt that Benji's pain was real, and she felt for him. She wasn't a coldhearted person, but she didn't have time to fall into another case, not even one that would surely prove relatively benign. She needed to work on her book. If she gave in to Joseph Macklin, when would it stop? She was done with hands-on therapy for the time being. She would help people through her books and that would have to be enough. Virtually any therapist she knew could help the child.

"I'll be away from New York for the next few months," she said. "So I'm in no position to begin a new therapy relationship, even if I wanted to."

"I'll bring Benji to you," the man said, surprising her. He had no idea where she was going. How could he insist he'd follow her without any sign of doubt in his voice?

"I'm heading to Japan," she lied.

"Good thing Benji has a passport." He smiled easily. "So do I, and a change of scenery could be good for us both."

"I'm not going to Japan." She studied him, still unsure how to approach the problem and make him go away. "It will be a substantial drive to reach my location. I assume Benji is afraid of cars now."

He shook his head. "He was at first, but now he's fine. He doesn't act nervous or afraid anytime we travel in my SUV. We will go wherever is necessary."

Something about him told her that it would be far easier and less time-consuming to give in to him. "Fine." She pulled a pen from her purse, then snatched back the business card she'd handed him, flipping it over to scribble down an address, date, and time. "As I said, I won't be in the city at all for the next few months. If you want me to see Benji, you'll have to come to me. Don't be late." She thrust the card at him. "I won't answer the door if you are."

He gaped at the address. "That's out in the boonies of Pennsylvania."

"I thought you were willing to go to Japan," she said, barely repressing the urge to smirk. "Pennsylvania is practically next door in comparison. But I can understand your reluctance to make the drive. It is lengthy and difficult to reach. Call my assistant, and she will give you that list of names I mentioned. Several are located in Manhattan, and you can reach them easily on the subway. No long drive necessary."

They locked eyes again, iron will against iron will. The big man folded first, but instead of saying he'd call her assistant as she expected, he simply said, "Fine." He dipped into his jacket pocket again, the one that had held Benji's drawing, and pulled out a business card. The print was stark and brief: *Macklin Security* in bold blue print, along with a phone number. Above the name and phone number was a logo, a stylized letter *M* that vaguely resembled an eye. "That's my firm, if you need to reach me."

"Thank you."

"Benji and I will be at the appointment on time."

Sure you will. Again Ginny suppressed a smirk. The road to her family's cabin was treacherous, with switchbacks and blind curves. Her father had counted on the difficulty in reaching the cabin to keep away the shadow government he believed was out to get him and his family. The malignant group he'd feared so deeply had existed only in his mind.

She might have found the one scenario in which the family paranoia could work in her favor. He would wander around the Pennsylvania forests and eventually give up and go home to the city. He'd choose one of the fine therapists readily available to his troubled nephew. Their current conversation would be the last she saw of Mr. Joseph Macklin.

Despite the gorgeous day, Mac was tired of driving through the woods. Trees loomed beside the narrow road as if intent on blocking the warm spring sunshine. The forest was a mixture of hardwoods and pines—mostly beech, birch, sugar maple, Canadian hemlock, and white pine, with a scattering of shorter trees including witch hazel and American holly taking advantage of any chance to catch the sunshine near the edge of the road. The result was that the road felt mysterious and dark.

He glanced sideways at Benji. Benji wore a slightly faded sweatshirt that had once been black but now had a slightly purple cast to it, and a peeling decal featuring a team of comic book superheroes. The boy had seen the shirt in the window of a vintage shop one day when he'd been out on a walk with Mac. He'd stopped and stared at the shirt without speaking, not asking for it or even pointing at it. But he'd shown an interest, so Mac had bought it. So few things caught Benji's attention since the accident.

Mac knew that letting a child ride in the front seat, even in the pricey booster he'd installed, wasn't as safe as putting him in the back, but Benji wasn't quite as relaxed in cars as Mac had implied to Dr. Bryce. The boy was fine in the front seat, but it was clear the back seat scared him, too similar to the day he'd lost his parents.

"You okay, buddy?" Mac asked.

Benji shifted position to peer up at his uncle with his huge brown eyes, his mother's eyes. In the weeks since his parents had died, the boy had lost some weight, growing smaller until his face was hauntingly gaunt. The boy's mop of dark hair needed a trim. Not long before the accident, Benji's mom had said something about getting Benji a haircut. It still hadn't happened, and Mac felt a fresh pang of guilt. What was he doing with a kid? His brother was the one who was good with kids, good with everyone, really. Mac felt as if he were flailing around in the dark, and it was a new sensation for him—one he did not enjoy.

Benji had studied Mac for a long while without acknowledging anything Mac said, but he didn't act distressed. After a while, he shifted in his seat to stare out the window again.

"It shouldn't be much longer," Mac said. "I'm surprised we haven't seen a deer yet." Benji didn't bother to acknowledge any of that and merely stared out the window. "If you see one, you gotta let me know. I haven't seen a deer in years. They aren't exactly prancing past the apartment."

His jovial tone felt strange in his mouth. He was putting too much effort into it. He wondered if Benji heard that. The boy had always been bright, something Mac's brother often bragged about. "He's intuitive too," Derrick had said more than once. "Same as his mother."

Thoughts of his brother and sister-in-law nudged the grief that lurked in Mac's chest all the time. He hadn't had much time for grief, throwing all his efforts into the funeral and then into helping Benji. He suspected the good Dr. Bryce wouldn't be complimentary about his strategy of stuffing down painful emotions.

Mac had an alarming thought. What if Dr. Bryce expected to administer some kind of family therapy where Mac plumbed the depths of his grief too? That was not something he was prepared for.

Anything for Benji, he reminded himself, a thought that had become almost a mantra.

"You're going to like Dr. Bryce," Mac said cheerfully, though he had no idea if it were true. Dr. Virginia Bryce was beautiful—there was no question of that—but she'd struck Mac as cold and unfriendly.

He almost questioned whether she could be the person he'd read such glowing things about. She had become a minor New York City celebrity when she got through to a badly abused child found wandering alone in the subway. That child had been unable to speak too. But Dr. Bryce had reached through the pain and led the child out into the world again. The things that child had told the police had no doubt prevented more children from being abducted and had likely saved lives.

Dr. Bryce was so acclaimed that she'd appeared on the cover of a popular New York magazine. During his research, Mac had read that article. The writer had gushed about Dr. Bryce's ability to connect with even the most broken children. Surely that meant she had a good heart buried beneath that stubborn persona. But would such a woman have refused Benji point-blank the way she had? The refusal had stung. Mac knew he sometimes had trouble giving up his first impressions of a person. He'd have to try harder, for Benji.

His eyes flicked to the clock. He was fairly confident they'd make it by the appointment time, which was a relief. He wanted to think Dr. Bryce wouldn't refuse to help Benji once she'd seen him, but he didn't know her well enough to test the theory.

"Dr. Bryce will be surprised," Mac said. "I think she expected me to get lost."

Benji's attention flashed to him, his expression filled with concern.

"We're not lost," Mac assured him. "I promise." Not that the trek hadn't been challenging. The narrow dirt road they were driving didn't even exist on most maps. The GPS on Mac's phone had given up offering any useful advice nearly an hour before. But Mac had expected that. He never went into any situation unprepared, so he'd both studied road maps to plan the route and tracked down topographical maps and even satellite imagery. As a result, there had been no surprises on the drive. He assumed that his passion for research and preparation was something the doctor had not counted on, and he almost chuckled at the thought of having bested her, suspecting that didn't happen often.

But then he glanced at Benji, who was gazing out the window again. The dark curls of the boy's hair brushed the frayed sweatshirt neckline, and something about the sight made Mac's heart ache all over again. How had Derrick and Madison trusted him with their amazing child? Surely he wasn't their only option. Surely they had friends who were more fatherly, more experienced.

He focused on the road again, blinking away the tears that threatened. His brother had trusted Mac with the most important person in his world, and Mac was going to live up to that trust. All that mattered was Benji, and the sunny child locked inside that silent imitation of him.

3

The smell of warm cookies filled the kitchen as Ginny opened the oven and pulled out a pan. To Ginny, that smell was key to what she imagined as a normal childhood. It was one of the reasons she often offered freshly baked cookies to her patients. The sense of smell was one of the most emotionally evocative, and she found it helped calm anxious children.

The fact that she'd made cookies was not proof that she'd given up on the idea of never seeing Joseph Macklin again. She still clung to hope that the man would get good and lost, drive around a while, then give up and go home, but every time she entertained the thought, she remembered the resolve on his face and a sliver of that hope eroded.

She slid the cookies from the parchment-lined pan to a cooling rack, intending to leave them for a few minutes before carrying a plateful to the rough-hewn table in the great room. Despite her hope that she'd spend the day alone, she would finish her preparations for Benji's arrival. She had no intention of making the boy wait or feel as if he were inconveniencing her in any way. The child had been through enough and didn't need to sense the slightest rejection from her.

Even if Benji and his uncle did show up, she doubted she'd have many sessions with the boy. His uncle would tire of the long drive and take his nephew to one of the other perfectly competent therapists in New York, and she would be left in peace. But until that happened, she would do her best to help Benji begin the healing process.

Ginny spun the vintage diving watch on her arm and saw that it was nearly time for them to arrive—assuming they'd be punctual, which wasn't likely. She stood still and absorbed the profound quiet of the cabin, a quiet she rarely experienced in the city. Outside, nature made its own noise. If she flung open the door, she'd hear birdsong and endless rustling in the woods that made up most of her property, but those more furtive sounds couldn't penetrate the thick glass of her windows or the log walls.

On the inside, it was nearly impossible to tell the cabin was built of logs. She'd had the interior reclad during the extensive remodel, wanting nothing about the place to remind her of her childhood. For a time, she'd considered tearing it down and building something modern and bright in its place, but that would have been wasteful, and Ginny wasn't a wasteful person. The cabin was well built and meticulously maintained. Tearing it down was an indulgence she couldn't justify, no matter how much she hated the memories in the walls.

Instead, she'd transformed it, much as she'd transformed her own life. The great room was spacious, bright, and full of beautiful things. It was the home she wished it had been all those years ago. She was still standing in the middle of the great room, hands on her hips, when the sound of tires biting into gravel distracted her. She groaned. Mr. Macklin had found his way to her house after all.

She scanned the room one final time, then strode to the front door. She grabbed her tweed blazer from the gnarled wood hall tree and pulled it on. The blazer was part of the trappings of academia, a kind of armor, and she wanted all the authority she could put on before dealing with Benji's formidable uncle.

She tugged the hem straight and smoothed the soft fabric, then opened the door as the tall man helped the child out of the SUV. The boy peered around curiously. That was a good sign. He was engaging with his surroundings. She'd worked with children in the past who were so deeply sunk into their pain that a new setting didn't even register.

When Benji and his uncle reached the door, Ginny focused on the boy, greeting him warmly. "Welcome, Benji. I'm glad to meet you. I'm Dr. Bryce, but it's okay with me if you call me Ginny. Would you care to come in?"

She saw Benji sniff and knew the scent of baking had wafted past her through the open door. "I have cookies." She eyed the tall man, who continued to watch the boy. "Benji doesn't have any food allergies, does he?"

The man shook his head. "No, and those cookies smell great."

"They are," she said. "Now, you may stay out here, Mr. Macklin. I need to be alone with Benji for the first session. If that's okay with you, Benji." She met the boy's eyes, and he made no particular response to the implied question in her words. "Come in, please."

She waited, holding her breath to see what Benji did next. There was a chance he'd cling to his uncle, a familiar buoy in the chaos that had taken over his life. But though the small boy appeared as fragile as dandelion fluff, he never hesitated, walking through the door and into the cabin with no sign of discomfort.

"I'll let you know when we're done." She stared at the tall man, expecting him to protest being left outside on the chilly spring day, but Mr. Macklin simply tipped his head at her.

"Thank you," he said seriously. "Thank you for seeing Benji. And you can call me Mac."

"No promises on either count," she said, then closed the door. She had to give him credit—apparently he'd meant it when he said he'd do anything for his nephew. Her opinion of him went up a notch. When Benji's session was over, she might even let Mac have a cookie.

After a tour of the cabin to help Benji relax and feel comfortable in the unfamiliar space, she asked him to take a seat at the table. She sat beside him in another chair, watching his reaction to judge if her physical closeness disturbed him. He swung his legs and munched on a cookie, appearing relaxed and heartwarmingly normal. Yet he hadn't made a sound.

Ginny began to explain the goals of therapy. "I want to help you deal with all the big, scary feelings," she said. "You don't have to talk. You don't have to do anything at all. You can spend your time here in any way you want. You can decide you just want to have cookies and enjoy the woods. Whatever you decide is how we'll proceed."

Benji gave her his full attention, eyes wide. She unfolded the drawing she'd gotten from his uncle. "This is pretty scary," she said. "Is it a picture of your uncle Mac?"

Benji blinked in surprise at the question and shook his head.

Ginny felt like cheering. It was the first direct response she'd gotten to a question. "I'm glad. Your uncle strikes me as a good guy who cares about you a lot."

Benji didn't respond, but some of the distress smoothed from his face.

"Is the scary man someone you know?" Ginny asked.

Benji's eyes flitted to the paper, then he ducked his head and shivered. Finally he did something that sent a shiver down Ginny's spine as well. He raised his eyes to Ginny again and pressed his finger to his lips in a soundless shushing gesture.

Ginny opened her mouth to ask if the scary man was a secret.

Instead, she jumped at the sound of gunshots outside.

One of the cabin windows shattered. Ginny threw herself over the child as another window blew out. They needed to get away from the windows. She knew the thick walls wouldn't allow anything less than a rocket to pass, but the windows were a dangerous weakness.

Ginny rushed Benji into the kitchen, keeping both of them low to avoid the line of the windows. The thick cabinets on the kitchen walls would offer even more protection, and the kitchen didn't have any windows. Once they were crouching next to a cabinet, Benji clung to her hand as Ginny ran through options in her mind. Someone, or perhaps more than one person, was outside, shooting. She didn't know the condition of Benji's uncle. Assuming he couldn't hold off armed men for long, the shooters would soon infiltrate the cabin.

She could take the boy out of the cabin. She didn't have a second door, but she did have a bulletproof window in her bedroom that could be swung open to allow easy exit, and they could escape through that. The window had cost her as much as the kitchen remodel, and she'd thought the purchase extravagant at the time, but it meant she would never be trapped in her bedroom.

She reluctantly discarded the idea of leaving through the window. Without knowing what was going on outside, she and Benji might walk right into the path of the gunmen.

Fortunately, the window wasn't her only way of getting out of the house, and the second option—the one she wasn't yet willing to consider—would keep them out of the gunmen's sight. But it came with its own problems.

Grimly, she decided it was safer inside for the moment. The cabin was basically a fortress and most of the windows in the house were far too small to allow anyone to climb through, even with the glass broken out. The real problem was that the front door wasn't locked.

"Benji, stay right here," she said firmly. "I have to lock the front door."

Benji shook his head, his grip tightening on Ginny's hand. Ginny could guess his line of thought. His uncle was out there where people were shooting. Benji didn't want him locked out. Ginny wasn't overly comfortable with the idea either.

"Okay, I won't lock the door. But I do need to find out what's going on outside, and I need you to stay here because it's the safest spot."

Benji pressed his lips together. Obviously he wasn't enthusiastic about that idea either, but he must have considered it the better of two options because he released her hand and wrapped both arms around his knees.

She realized with a jolt that he was reliving the trauma of the crash that had taken his parents. How could she leave him in such a state?

It was clear. She couldn't. Whatever happened, she would stay with him.

———♡———

Hunched behind his SUV, Mac felt the urge to pound his fist against the vehicle door in frustration. He was desperate to get inside the cabin. It appeared solid enough, but he'd heard the windows shatter. Mac had noticed when they pulled up that the front cabin windows were oddly shaped—tall and narrow—but they didn't stop bullets. Benji could already be hurt, already bleeding. Mac might be too late, might fail his nephew again, and in the worst way possible.

He checked to see how many shots he had left. *Two. Great.*

"I have to get in there," he muttered. Nothing else was acceptable. Inside, he could put himself between his nephew and whoever was shooting at them. Out here, he was lightly armed with no extra ammunition and almost no information. He was fairly sure bullets were coming from two different directions, but he hadn't seen either of the shooters yet. Still, he popped up and sent his last two bullets in the direction of the previous fire and ran toward the door. With each pounding step he expected to feel the burn of a bullet ripping into him, but he made it through the cabin door.

"Virginia!" he bellowed as he shoved the empty gun into a holster under his jacket. "Benji!"

"In the kitchen," Dr. Bryce called back. "We're okay. Stay away from the windows."

I'm not an idiot, he thought rebelliously.

"Stay there." Mac locked the door behind him, then shoved three dead bolts into place as he heard bullets thudding into the door. For a split second, he wondered why Dr. Bryce had so many locks, but then he discarded the thought, glad she did. Three dead bolts would slow up anyone unwelcome who tried to get in.

He hunched low and ran for the kitchen, crouching past the windows. A bullet whizzed over his bent head, but he kept moving and soon reached the others in the kitchen. He checked Benji over, grateful to see the boy showed no sign of actual injury. His gaze shifted to the doctor, and he was not overly surprised that she was completely calm.

"We have to get out of here," he said, his voice low. "I assume there's another door."

"Not exactly."

Worry launched him directly into exasperation. "What does that mean?"

"It means I don't have another door," Dr. Bryce said, her voice tight. "But I do have another way out." She nudged Benji toward his uncle.

"I need my hands free," Mac said. "There are at least two shooters out there. Eventually they'll try to get in here, and those broken windows will make handy entrances."

"They're too narrow for an adult even with the glass broken out," Dr. Bryce said. "They're custom. Still, I agree—they'll find a way in eventually. That means you need to let me get us out of here. But I need you to take care of Benji." She nudged the boy toward him, then crawled across the kitchen floor and stood.

Mac looked toward the large great room, but he could see her present position wouldn't be visible from the front windows. How had she known that? *Surely this isn't something she planned for. Who is this woman?*

Dr. Bryce wrenched open a door in the kitchen wall, beyond which was a large pantry. The walls were lined with shelves and food. "Come here," she commanded. "Stay low."

Benji lurched toward the pantry, but Mac held him tightly. "We don't need a place to hide," he said. "We need an exit."

"I know. Come in here, now."

With no other plans, Mac let Benji go so he could crawl to the pantry. Maybe there was a panic room in there. That, at least, would give them a place to hide until the men outside grew tired of trying to kill them. He crawled along behind the boy until they were all inside the pantry.

"Close the door, but stay close to it," the woman said, her back toward them. She was hauling a duffel bag down from a shelf and setting it heavily on the floor. The bag had hidden a keypad from view. She punched in a number, and a click drew Mac's attention to the floor. A section of the wooden floor popped open.

Dr. Bryce shoved several bags of flour in front of the keypad, hiding it once more. "Now you see why I didn't call it a door," she said.

Mac reached down and lifted the wooden hatch. Below it was absolute darkness. "What's down there?"

"Our way out." She dropped the duffel through the hole, then sat down with her legs dangling into the darkness.

"Wait a second," Mac demanded, not liking how fast everything had been taken out of his hands. "You have a secret tunnel?"

"Indirectly. It belonged to my father." Then without another word, she scooted forward and dropped into the darkness. He heard her hit the ground with a grunt. A dim light flickered to life below them, and Mac could see Dr. Bryce's arms reaching up. "Hand me Benji."

Mac didn't approve of anything he'd seen in the last several minutes, but with his choices so limited, he didn't bother arguing. He peered into his nephew's eyes. "You okay?" To his surprise, Benji nodded. "Good. You ready?"

Benji scooted toward the hole.

Mac caught him under the arms and handed him down until he felt Dr. Bryce take the boy's weight from below. "You guys clear?" he asked.

"Clear," she said. "Come on down."

Mac did, dropping into the hole feet first. He expected to hit some kind of dirt floor, assuming the pit was an old-fashioned root cellar dug out under the cabin, but the floor was hard. Someone had put a lot of work into building it. He couldn't begin to guess why.

Mac scanned the area around him as best he could, but could see virtually nothing. The lone light source was the sickly green of a chemical glow stick Dr. Bryce held in one hand. She stepped closer to the wall and pressed a button. The overhead hatch closed, making the dark tunnel even darker. She scooped up her duffel and handed the glow stick to Benji. "Can you handle being in charge of our light?"

He nodded solemnly, gazing at the glow stick.

"I don't think those guys are going to give up easily," Mac said. "They will find this place eventually." He immediately regretted the remark, his attention shifting to Benji. He didn't want to scare the child more than he already was.

"That's why we have to keep moving," the psychologist said. She hefted the duffel bag high on her shoulder. "Follow me."

"If you're leading," Mac said, "shouldn't you hold the light?"

"I don't need it, and it'll help you and Benji."

She had already started off and would disappear out of the limited range of the light if they didn't get moving. Benji took Mac's hand and tugged on it, clearly wanting to stay close to Dr. Bryce. Mac had read patients tended to bond with their therapists, but he suspected the events since they arrived had sped things up considerably.

With Benji tugging on his hand, Mac followed. He didn't have the faintest clue where they were headed and was slightly unnerved that a child psychologist had an escape shaft out of her home, but since they didn't have many options, he swallowed his questions and trailed behind his nephew. For now, he'd follow blindly in order to get Benji to safety, but eventually he would expect some answers from the peculiar woman leading them down a dark tunnel.

4

Though the glow stick's dim light stretched far enough to reach Ginny as she led Mac and Benji through the tunnel, the darkness ahead remained impenetrable. For the first time in her life, Ginny was grateful that she knew the tunnel. Not from recent use, but there had been a time when navigating its path was essential for her survival—or so she'd been told.

Ginny saw the green glow brightening right before a small hand slipped into hers. Benji held up the light stick, and Ginny could see that the chemical luminescence had already begun to fade. It should have lasted longer, but she hadn't kept up the contents of the go bag the way she'd been taught. She'd no longer believed it was necessary or even sane to put so much thought into escaping from her own home. Her mouth twisted in a wry smile. *Score one for Dad.*

"Benji," she said, making sure her voice was quiet and completely calm. "That glow stick is going to run out before we reach the end of the tunnel. That's probably going to be scary, but you don't have to worry. I know this tunnel." She studied his small face. "Do you understand?"

He raised those big eyes toward her, his face serious but not fearful. He was a tough kid. She squeezed his hand, and they continued walking. Ginny was surprised she hadn't gotten more questions and demands from Benji's uncle. He didn't strike her as the sort to relinquish control without comment.

Ginny reached out with the hand that wasn't holding Benji's, shifting until she touched the wall of the tunnel. The wall was damp.

She'd expected as much since she could hear the distant sound of trickling water. That was new. Her father would not have allowed that. He'd often talked about the destructive force of water. "It worms its way into man-made things," he'd told her once. "Humans only win against nature if we stay vigilant."

Ginny shook her head. Leave it to her father to turn water into an enemy. Not for the first time, she thought he would have been a therapist's nightmare.

On the other hand, her father's paranoia might have saved their lives. Ginny would never have paid to put a tunnel under her holiday cabin. But the cabin had never been a holiday spot for her father. It had been a true retreat, a place to hide from a world that he believed had grown feral. Her father had blown through the bulk of his wealthy wife's money creating the perfect shrine to fear. And once it was built, he'd hauled Ginny and her mother out into the woods and spent hours drilling them on how to survive.

Ginny thought she'd put those days behind her. She'd even considered blocking off the tunnel, a final proof that she wasn't the wacky survivalist's daughter anymore, but she hadn't quite been able to go that far. She could almost hear her father's rough voice in her head as if he could see her now. *Guess I wasn't as nutty as you thought.*

"I guess not, Dad," she whispered, barely a breath, but louder than she'd intended in the quiet of the tunnel. Benji squeezed her fingers again.

"Where does this tunnel go?" Mac's voice was quiet and closer than she'd expected. Her woolgathering had weakened her situational awareness, and she hadn't noticed him closing the space between them.

She swallowed, pushing down her self-recrimination over the distraction. "To a second cabin," she answered. "It's much smaller and about a quarter mile from mine."

"A quarter mile?" Mac's voice reflected his astonishment. "This tunnel is a quarter of a mile long?"

Ginny almost laughed. She considered telling him that her father hadn't believed in doing something unless he overdid it. Instead, she said, "We shouldn't talk more than necessary. There are air vents to the surface. They can carry sound as well."

"I assumed as much," he said. But that was all. He didn't ask questions about why she had a tunnel in the first place or whether she knew who the shooters might be.

She didn't know, and it bothered her. If it hadn't been decades since her parents' deaths, she would believe the shooters were after her father. No one that paranoid managed to go through life without making enemies, but it made no sense for anyone to show up when her father had been gone for so long.

Were they after her? She received hate mail and even the occasional threat. Therapists who dealt with the kind of trauma Ginny did and who worked with the police as often as she had in the past collected hate mail almost as a matter of course. Plus, Ginny was almost a celebrity. But she couldn't imagine anyone coming out to her cabin. Even if someone hated her, how would they have found her all the way out in the sticks?

Ginny could hear Mac's footsteps behind her. She had an exact picture of how far away he was based on the sound. She would prefer that he didn't follow quite so close, but with his nephew's hand in hers, she understood.

She had done her homework on Joseph Macklin after meeting him. She had invited him to visit her cabin, and she didn't take that lightly. So she'd learned everything she could, mostly through the impressive research skills and caution of Willow.

Benji's uncle had no military experience, which had surprised her. He moved as if he had military training. He'd also never been a policeman, another past career that might have explained his manner. What he had, astonishingly enough, was a former baseball career—or the beginning of one, before an injury had put a stop to it. Apparently the rest of his skill set was self-taught.

She was impressed by the idea of a self-made security man. Her dad would have loved the guy. Her father also had no military or police training, but he'd instructed his family with the relentlessness of a hardnosed drill sergeant. And she knew from experience that a person could learn and accomplish astonishing things with the right motivation.

She pushed thoughts of her family aside and kept running through what she knew about the man behind her. The ex-ballplayer had launched a security firm with his brother, Derrick, who did have a background in military intelligence. Apparently Derrick had been gifted when it came to computers and security.

The firm had one additional partner, a man named Calvin Burfield, who wasn't related to Mac and Derrick. In the firm's photo, Calvin seemed small and slender next to the two brothers but possessed the same easy, confident grin.

Willow had also dug up newspaper clippings about the car accident that had killed Derrick and his wife, Madison. A photo of the damaged car had made Ginny shudder in horror that Benji had been trapped in a vehicle that sustained so much damage. According to the report, he'd waited hours for rescue. She had to give him credit. He'd been through a lot, but here he was, trooping through a tunnel at her side, without so much as a whimper of complaint.

"What's in the bag?" Mac asked, almost in her ear. At least she'd been aware of his movement and didn't jump.

"Food," she said. "Water—though not a lot—plastic sheeting, a fire starter, a filter bottle, first aid supplies, a knife." She decided he didn't actually need a list, so she broke off with a shrug. "Useful things."

"Were the men at the cabin after you?" he asked. She felt his breath slightly behind her ear and shivered.

The automatic rejection of the idea died on her lips. Hadn't she been thinking about the ugly mail she'd gotten? She'd been responsible for a number of arrests, for the removal of children from abusive families. She believed the number of people who hated her was small, but they were motivated. And as she'd just been thinking, people could do nearly anything with enough motivation.

"I don't think so, but it isn't impossible. Therapists make people angry sometimes. But those men showed up right after you arrived. Isn't it more plausible that they were following you, especially since my cabin is so hard to find? I can't imagine the security business doesn't upset people now and then."

He didn't answer right away, and Ginny was fine with that. They shouldn't be talking. Not only could the vents carry sound out to the woods, but she should be listening, not letting her thoughts run around like puppies at a park. The vents carried sounds from the woods, and she'd been paying them no attention at all.

"We should listen for movement above us," she said softly.

"Could you tell whether the movement belongs to people or animals?" Mac asked.

Could she ever. Her father's training sessions had often involved the tunnel. She could run through it in the pitch darkness and never fall or hit a wall. But she could also listen. Many times, her father had demanded she report what she heard. Once she'd heard something crashing through the woods over her head and imagined a monster. Her father had laughed at her. He told her she'd heard a deer, or maybe a bear. There were no monsters in the woods.

But there could be on her journey with Mac and Benji.

Mac backed off slightly, sensing the doctor's discomfort at his presence so close behind her, and he mused on her question. Could the men outside be after him? The timing had been suspicious. If their target was indeed Dr. Bryce, why wait until she had company instead of hitting her when she was alone? And he knew that his work sometimes involved secrets. Secrets someone might kill for.

But why now? He wasn't working because his focus had been on Benji's needs. That also meant he carried considerably less weaponry than usual. The more he thought about it, the more he understood why a killer might think it was a good time to go after him.

He growled softly under his breath. The trip into the wilds of the Pennsylvania mountains must have been quite a gift to the shooters. No wonder they'd struck. There would never be a better, more private place to take him out. That meant he'd dragged Benji from the safety of their NYC apartment and shoved him and the doctor into danger.

Though he was beginning to think Dr. Virginia Bryce was better able to handle the unexpected situation than he could have imagined. She was unflinchingly calm. And a quarter mile of underground? He could barely believe it. The tunnel smelled damp, but the floor was even and the walls were smooth and slightly curving. As far as he could tell, it was a single straight shot with no side tunnels, though that was hard to judge in the darkness.

He closed the distance between himself and the therapist again. "I think the glow stick is fading. Do you have a flashlight in that bag?" He could use his phone as a flashlight, but he didn't want to burn through the battery. He couldn't get a signal, but that didn't mean it wouldn't save their lives later.

"I do," she said. "But we may need it a lot more later. I know this tunnel well. I could make it with no light at all. I'll get out another glow stick if Benji gets scared, but he's doing great so far."

"He's a superhero," Mac said, though he hated that his young nephew had to be tough or brave. He should be home with Derrick and Madison, giggling and watching cartoons or tossing a ball around.

"He is."

Mac reached out and caught the doctor's arm. She gasped at the contact but didn't jerk away. "What?"

"How deep is this tunnel?"

"I'm not completely sure," she said. "I was really young when it was built. But I've been through it countless times and it stays pretty level."

"Yeah," he said. "I noticed that. Hold on. Let me try my phone."

"You still have your phone?" Her tone was sharp. "That's not smart. That could be how they followed you."

"My phone is secure. It's possible someone put a tracker on the SUV. I've gotten out of the habit of sweeping for tracking devices since I haven't been working."

Mac pulled the phone from his pocket and the screen lit up. The light shone almost blindingly bright in the tunnel.

"I still wish you'd ditched it," she said and the chill of her disapproval couldn't have been clearer.

He didn't respond to that as he peered at the phone screen. He still had no service, but it was possible that would change once they weren't below ground. They'd come out eventually and he could make a call. Until then, they were on their own and a long way from help.

"No signal," he admitted.

"Then shut it off," she said. "If they are tracking you, we don't need a homing beacon."

"Maybe I want the light." He knew that sounded childish, but he bristled at her tone. He knew about phones and tracking. He was the security expert. It didn't help that what she'd said was exactly what he intended to do. He wouldn't refuse simply to spite her, but he could do without the commanding tone.

"Fine." She unzipped the duffel and rooted around inside. She pulled out a flashlight and handed it to him. "Now will you shut off the phone?"

He did, already regretting his stubbornness. It wasn't the time or place to play games, though something about her small concession made him feel better all the same. He'd have to watch that. He'd seen plenty of team efforts crash and burn because team members wanted to play king of the castle instead of working together.

Mac shone the flashlight around the tunnel. The beam reached farther than the weak light of Benji's glow stick, and Mac froze at what he saw up ahead. "What's that?"

"I'm not sure," the doctor admitted.

He kept the light aimed ahead as they picked up speed. They soon reached the spot Mac had seen. The tunnel had caved in. It was completely blocked by dirt, stones, and broken hunks of concrete pipe.

Their escape tunnel had reached a dead end.

5

"This is bad." Mac played the flashlight beam over the rubble in front of them. "This is too much to dig out before the shooters figure out where we are and come after us."

Ginny felt the alarm from Mac's words pass through Benji's hand, which finally began to tremble in hers. "In that case," she said, keeping her voice completely calm. "We'll need to do something different."

As a child, she'd never once thought about how the tunnel must have been made. It had simply existed, and she'd run through it a few times a day in the pitch dark. She could see the broken hunks of cement pipe in the debris. Water must have been working against the pipe for decades, probably helped along by tree roots. Without her father's constant patrol of the ground over the pipe, nature had found a way in.

But that offered a new possibility. "Can you shine your light above us?" He did, and she saw the tangle of roots and where they'd pushed through a sizeable break in the pipe. "Shut off the light."

To his credit, he did what she said instantly and without question. She had been staring up at the roof and when the light went off, she waited patiently for her eyes to adjust to the lack of light. That was when she saw it. A tiny gap in the ceiling of the tunnel, at the edge of the cave-in, let in a bright beam of light. "Can you see the light?" she asked him.

"Yeah." Mac moved, the sound of his footsteps loud in the tunnel, and the light disappeared. "We could dig this out if we had the right tools."

"Good." She squeezed Benji's hand, then let it go so she could root through her duffel. She easily found what she wanted. "I have a camping shovel. It's not large, but it's a good one." The tool was designed for digging impromptu latrines or putting out a fire safely.

The flashlight came on, offering a clear view of the camping shovel as she screwed the pieces together. "I assume that is part of the stuff you mentioned."

"I put a lot of thought into being prepared." She tightened all the connections and then held out the shovel. "How about we trade, Mr. Macklin? I imagine you'll shovel us out quicker than I could. You're taller for one thing. I can hold the light for you."

The light tilted toward the floor as he handed it over. "Please call me Mac," he said. "Surely a near-death experience moves us beyond the 'mister' phase."

She didn't respond but took the light and used it to guide the shovel into his hand.

In a wry voice, he said, "Thank you, Dr. Bryce."

"I suppose you can call me Ginny," she said, knowing her grudging tone bordered on rude, but nothing about the day she'd had so far was making her feel particularly friendly. And she wasn't sure that it wasn't at least partially his fault.

"Thank you, Ginny," he said, the words considerably warmer. He got to work on the hole.

She held the light carefully so that it illuminated the ceiling but avoided blinding him as he worked. Benji stayed close to her side, no longer holding her hand, but close enough that he could lean on her if he chose.

Ginny was impressed with how quickly Mac widened the tiny gap into a sizeable opening. She had no doubt that she could have dug them out, but not nearly as quickly. He was strategic in a way that impressed her. Soon she realized he was not only widening the hole, but he was also moving the dirt and broken pipe to make a slope they could climb to reach the hole once he was done.

"That's it," he said finally. "There's a huge tree root, and I can't chop through it with this shovel. So we'll have to squeeze between the edge of the pipe and the tree root. You go first, Ginny. Then I'll hand Benji up."

She examined the hole critically. "You won't fit."

"I will. I'll have to."

He had a point. Debate and discussion wouldn't get them out. So she nudged Benji closer to his uncle. She considered saying something comforting to the child, but nothing came to mind, so she merely touched his shoulder before beginning the scramble up, shifting debris to reach the cavity.

The rubble was rough under her hands, but Ginny paid scant attention to it. Instead, she considered possible ways to widen the gap as she pushed through. She was relieved to find it wasn't as tight as she'd expected, but Mac was a big guy. It wouldn't be easy for him.

She climbed part of the way through before pausing to check her surroundings, caution ingrained in her. The sinkhole where the pipe had collapsed was almost hidden by deadfall. The roots of a fallen spruce tree reached toward her in a tangle. It was probably the tree that had caused the break in the pipe in the first place. At least no one searching for them in the woods was likely to find it.

She scanned the woods as far as she could see in every direction, listening. She heard birds rustling among the leaves nearby, and they wouldn't be doing that if hunters were tramping through the trees nearby. She hauled herself the rest of the way out but stayed low, lying on her belly. She shifted her position to reach back the way she'd come, thrusting her arms into the hole.

She didn't speak. There was no telling how far her voice would carry, but she assumed Mac would be smart enough to know what she wanted. Sure enough, he lifted Benji up, and the boy stretched his arms toward her. She inched forward, pushing herself with her toes, until she was gripping Benji's upper arms, then crawled backward, lifting him out.

As soon as he was out, he wriggled out of her arms and crawled out of the way. He sat among the tangle of roots, watching her intently. She gave him a thumbs-up. The little boy was doing far better than she could have hoped.

Ginny thrust her arms into the chasm once more.

"I can climb up on my own," Mac said.

Frustrated, Ginny risked a few low words. "The duffel."

"Right." He handed it up, and she scooted away from the hole with the bag hugged to her chest. Benji edged closer to her and leaned against her shoulder. She surprised herself by leaning over and kissing the boy on the top of his dusty head.

He peered up at her, unsmiling, but didn't seem to mind. His eyes shifted toward the opening, and together Ginny and Benji waited to see if Mac was going to fit through. Soft grunts and bits of debris flying into the air over the hole signaled his efforts. Then the shovel flew out, landing near Ginny's toes. She picked it up and held onto it.

One arm extended from the gap, then a head. Mac squirmed, breathing heavily. Ginny resisted the urge to reach forward and pull on his arm. If he wanted her help, he'd let her know. She imagined watching a wine cork try to work itself out of a bottle would go much the same way. Mac gained some ground but then simply thrashed without clear advancement. He was stuck.

Ginny crawled toward him. "Hold on." She began digging around him until she'd exposed the tree root that played the largest part in keeping him trapped. Then she used the edge of the shovel blade to chop tiny pieces off the root. It was slow going, and she had no idea how long the shovel would stand up under the abuse.

"Leave me."

She ignored him and dragged her bag close again. She rooted around in the contents and pulled out an impressive hunting knife. She'd paid a great deal for it and knew the blade was strong and sharp.

Mac's eyes widened at the sight of the blade, but he didn't comment as Ginny hacked at the root with the knife. Her progress was considerably quicker than with the shovel, but she had to take care. She was working close to Mac's neck and shoulder.

Finally she'd hacked enough off the root that she thought it might move. She set the knife to one side and pushed against the root with all her strength. She felt it bend under her hands. It didn't bow far, but she had to hope it would be enough. Mac began wriggling again, and to her relief, it was obvious that he was going to get out. In the end, he sprawled on the ground beside the hole, panting.

As Ginny repacked the knife and shovel in the bag, Benji crawled over to hug his uncle. Mac reacted with surprise at the display of affection, but he quickly hugged the boy in response.

When Ginny finished stowing the tools, Mac leaned over to speak in her ear. "Where is the tunnel exit?"

She took a moment to orient herself, then pointed.

"A straight shot?" he asked.

"Should be."

"Then let's go."

———♡———

Ginny got to her feet and hoisted the duffel up onto her shoulder, then took Benji's hand and helped him to his feet. The boy didn't resist, but he wobbled. Mac could see the child had nearly reached his limit.

He waved Ginny away and picked Benji up. He wasn't happy about the thought of not having both hands free, but they would move faster if Benji wasn't in danger of stumbling and falling from exhaustion. He didn't dare have Benji climb onto his back, afraid of making the boy an easy target if the gunmen spotted them.

Benji clung to Mac with his arms around Mac's neck and his legs wrapped as far around Mac's waist as he could reach. Mac settled the boy, then crouched and gestured for Ginny to head in the direction she'd pointed earlier, toward the tunnel's intended exit.

The forest around them fortunately had a limited amount of undergrowth. That made passing between the trees easier, but it didn't give them as much cover as he would have liked. As unpleasant as the dark tunnel had been, he found that he missed it, because exposure out in the open was so much more dangerous.

Mac knew it had to be late afternoon, and the shadows in the woods were deep and eerie. All around them he heard the soft rustle of birds and animals digging through the leaf litter that covered the ground. The air had the bite of decaying leaves and damp. When the dark moved in, the air would grow cold fast, on top of all their other problems.

On the other hand, the idea of living long enough to get cold probably ought to sound good to him.

Ahead of him, Ginny moved through the forest in virtual silence, which impressed him considerably. He wasn't faring nearly as well. Then again, he was carrying a small child and didn't know the area as well as she obviously did.

When he'd watched her lecture, he'd judged her as an academic, the quintessential city dweller. He would never have guessed that a woman who owned an escape tunnel lay hidden beneath her cool, sophisticated demeanor. *I underestimated her.*

He expected the trip through the forest to take longer than it ultimately did. Ginny held up a hand to stop him, then pointed ahead before stepping behind the thickest tree trunk. He stepped behind another even as he squinted ahead to see a tiny tumbledown cabin.

He watched the building for several minutes, alert to any sign of movement.

The place seemed deserted. But after the past hour, Mac didn't trust anything that appeared so innocuous.

Mac moved closer to Ginny and began to untangle his nephew so he could hand him over. "Let me check this out," he said softly. "You and Benji stay here."

As he'd expected, she scowled at the suggestion, but she didn't resist taking the boy. She cradled the child against her, and he clung to her, somehow fitting even better than he had on Mac. "I'll be back."

Mac walked away from the woman who had been virtually a stranger that morning, but whom he trusted with his nephew without hesitation. He moved from tree to tree, wishing his footsteps were as silent as Ginny's, but he settled for managing not to trod on many of the sticks littering the ground. The trek to the cabin, darting from tree to tree for cover, took longer than he'd expected, but when he finally reached the ramshackle structure, he was glad for the extra precaution.

The cabin wasn't empty. A man in a dark turtleneck, a bulletproof vest, and dark jeans was crouching on the rough floor of the small structure. A ragged rug lay in a pile beside the man, whose attention didn't waver from the hatch near his feet. He was waiting for them, which meant he knew about the tunnel, though not about the cave-in. Did that mean the shooters hadn't bothered to follow the trio into it?

Tactically, since they believed Mac was armed, it made more sense to simply wait at the ends of the tunnel. Mac, Ginny, and Benji would have to come up sometime, and whoever waited at the top would have the clear advantage—an advantage they might not have had in the tunnel.

Mac pressed his back to the wall and surveyed the surrounding woods. If the other shooter remained in Ginny's cabin, they were relatively safe among the trees, but it wasn't something they could count on for long. Eventually someone would go into the tunnel after them and find the cave-in, as well as the place where he, Ginny, and Benji had climbed out. Then they'd comb the woods. At least, that was what Mac would do in their circumstances.

As quietly as he'd approached the cabin, Mac retraced his steps to rejoin Ginny and Benji. He saw that the boy's eyes were closed and didn't open at Mac's approach. Mac leaned close and spoke in Ginny's ear. "Bad guy in the cabin. Any other ideas?"

She didn't immediately answer, which he respected. She didn't guess. He could see her mind at work behind her dark-green eyes. Finally she nodded slowly, though he could tell by her expression that she wasn't enthusiastic about whatever she had in mind.

She let go of Benji with one hand and pointed. Mac peered in the direction of her gesture. What was that way? A village? A road? A ranger station? He didn't dare ask since they couldn't risk a lengthy chat. All he could do was trust the woman. She knew the area better than he did, better than he would ever have guessed. She also understood the seriousness of their situation, so whatever she suggested would almost certainly make things better.

Except that Mac really didn't like the doubt in her eyes. Still, what choice did they have? They couldn't discuss it out in the open, within yards of a man with a gun and a bulletproof vest. With a slow exhalation, seeking a calmness he wasn't sure he'd find anytime soon, Mac held out his arms for Benji.

Ginny passed the boy to his uncle.

Then Mac inclined his head in the direction she'd pointed. *Lead on.*

So she did.

6

Mac knew Benji couldn't actually be getting heavier, but it felt as if he were. The steadily climbing terrain didn't make the journey any easier. The rule of thumb for being lost in the woods was to follow a stream or river downhill, not up, but he couldn't see any running water, and it was clear Ginny had a specific destination in mind.

Mac had never spent much time in the woods. He was the son of a cardiologist, not an outdoorsman. His dad had never had time for camping with his sons, and Mac's mother was no fonder of the idea, having considered the carefully-tended garden of their upscale Connecticut home as close to wilderness as she cared to venture. Mac and his brother had gone to summer camp every year, but Mac had always favored sports-related camps. Derrick and his best friend, Cal, had gone for the more traditional camping in the woods. Derrick had loved that sort of thing and had always returned home with stories about bears and canoes and hiking.

Mac had respected his brother's love of summer camp, but he hadn't been able to relate. It wasn't as if spending six weeks in the woods would make him better at baseball. Mac hefted Benji higher, hoping to relieve some of the pain in his shoulders as he mused that Derrick would have excelled in their situation, and not only because Derrick understood the woods. Derrick understood people better as well.

Benji's head bobbed slightly against Mac's chest as he walked. Though the boy kept his arms around Mac's neck, his grip loosened as he dozed. They needed rest and food, not to mention a chance to plan instead of simply reacting. Mac strained his eyes, hoping with each step that he'd spot a building, but all he saw were trees, which seemed to stretch on for miles.

Ahead of Mac, Ginny stopped suddenly and raised a hand, signaling for him to stop walking. He still didn't see anything but woods. Ginny dropped back and Mac bent to let her whisper in his ear. That shift of position with the boy in his arms caused his muscles to protest, but he refused to so much as wince.

"It's not far," Ginny whispered. "I'll take Benji. It'll be better if you scout the place, I think."

Not sure her belief in him was justified, Mac handed Benji over. The boy whimpered in his sleep, but kept his eyes closed, wrapping himself around Ginny instantly. She took his weight without bowing, but strain showed in her features. She was tired too. Mac felt a little glad to see a display of human frailty from the stoic psychologist.

"How far?" he murmured.

"You'll see it from the top of the rise," she said. Then she stepped away from him and put her shoulder against a wide oak, using it for support as she held the sleeping child.

Mac set off, still not entirely sure what he expected to see at the top of the rise. Without Benji's weight, he moved as quickly as possible while still taking care not to step on branches or push the brush to its breaking point.

At the top of the rise, he spotted a cabin. It was about the same size as Ginny's, but more modern, with lots of windows. The brush around the cabin needed trimming, but overall, it was probably a nice vacation spot. He moved closer.

The cabin door was closed, but the windows offered clear visibility inside. As far as he could see, there was no sign of activity and the door hadn't been forced open. Unlike Ginny's cabin, this one had two doors with the side door opening onto a small deck. Near the main cabin, a second outbuilding was even more overgrown and undisturbed. A gravel road wove between the two buildings and off into the woods.

Mac hurried back down the hill toward Ginny. "No one has been there."

"Good. I have a key."

He raised his eyebrows. How many cabins did she own? "It's yours?"

She shook her head but didn't offer further information.

Mac had expected her to hand Benji to him, so he was surprised when she stepped away from the tree and started up the rise, only mildly slowed down under Benji's weight. With her much-smaller size, she must feel the burden even more than Mac had, but if it bothered her, she didn't show it.

At the cabin's front door, Ginny put Benji down, holding him while he found his feet. He didn't fuss, though he blinked and rubbed his eyes with one hand, holding the other out to Mac. He took it while Ginny dug a ring of keys out of her blazer pocket. She found the key she wanted and let them into the cabin.

Though it felt good to be surrounded by walls again, Mac wasn't excited about all the windows. Whoever built the place must have enjoyed the broad forest view. Mac did not. At least most of the windows had thick drapes that obscured the glass, though that also meant the interior of the cabin was deeply shadowed.

"The cabin uses a generator for electricity," Ginny said, once the door was closed securely behind them. "But that's too noisy, so there won't be any power. Not that we'd want lights on anyway. Too many windows."

Benji tugged free of Mac's hand, and he let the boy go. "Who owns this place?"

"A lawyer from New York. He doesn't come out from the city nearly as often as I do, so I check on the place for him. There's a rainwater system on the roof, and it's gravity fed so there will be water to wash up. If you don't mind the cold since we can't power the water heater right now."

The thought wasn't appealing, but Mac didn't remark on it while he watched his nephew wander around, peering into corners and studying small decor objects without touching them.

"I don't suppose your lawyer friend has a satellite phone or maybe a radio transmitter of some sort?"

"Sorry," Ginny said. "That's the point behind these cabins—to get out of contact for a while."

Mac hadn't expected a different answer. "I'll go scout the area," he said. "I want to make sure no one is heading our way."

"Good plan," she said. "I'll see if I can fix us something to eat."

"Stay away from the windows," he said and almost chuckled at Ginny's expression. If she were slightly less self-disciplined, he felt certain she would have rolled her eyes.

Mac took a last look at his nephew, who was nose-to-nose with what Mac guessed was a taxidermy ferret. Ginny's lawyer friend had strange tastes. Then he ducked out the door, closing it quietly behind him.

Ginny saw Benji's eyes focus sharply on the door when Mac left. "He'll be okay," she assured the child. "You can poke around all you want, but stay inside and away from the windows."

Benji nodded, and Ginny was surprised at that small act of acknowledgment. He was becoming more comfortable with responding. He wasn't talking, but Ginny was growing more and more certain that she could help him, given the chance. The boy walked over to sit on a dark tweed sofa, where a single shaft of light from the window hit the small coffee table, and he began to leaf through the magazines scattered there.

Ginny headed into the kitchen area. As with her cabin, the place was mostly one large room with a separate bedroom and bathroom. That meant she could find something for them to eat while still being able to watch Benji.

She poked through the cupboards without hesitation. Anything they ate could be replaced easily enough. She found several cans of vegetables, a carton of broth, and even a large can of chicken. She should be able to pull together a decent pot of soup. It wouldn't be the best thing any of them had ever eaten, but it would be more filling than the granola bars in her duffel.

She hauled the duffel onto the counter and fished out the small camp stove from inside. It required butane to operate, so it wasn't the most practical item for use on the run. They wouldn't get more than one meal out of it, but she knew one hot meal could make a big difference in morale.

At least the camp stove didn't require electricity or a big fire, either of which could attract the shooters. Once they'd rested, they could head up to the ranger station at the top of the mountain. It was a serious hike, but they'd be able to contact the outside world from there.

Ginny emptied the cans into a pot she'd found in the cupboard and set it over the camp stove, then jumped when she felt a tug on her sleeve. She discovered Benji at her elbow, wearing an apologetic expression. "It's okay," she said. "Do you need something?"

He held up a long yellow legal pad and a pencil. Then pointed at himself.

"You want to draw something?"

He held up the pad again in response.

"That's fine." She wished she had crayons for him in the bag, but they weren't a priority in a go bag. It wasn't that crayons couldn't be useful. She knew several potential uses for them in survival situations. Of course she did. With her father as tutor, she knew the potential survival use of virtually everything. Wouldn't her dad gloat to know how much she needed that information now?

Benji carried the pad and pencil to a small table next to the kitchen.

Ginny frowned, wondering if the table was too close to the windows. She remembered how hard it had been to see through the glass when they'd approached and decided that Benji would be safe enough.

The soup bubbled in the pot and smelled far better than she would have thought possible, considering every ingredient came from a can. All the running around and fear for their lives had worked up quite an appetite. She rooted around the cupboards to see if she could find something to go with the soup. She found a metal tin of crackers that still broke with a snap.

As she set the tin on the counter, she heard a hiccup from the table where Benji was working. She rummaged in the bag for a bottle of water and started toward the table before she realized the hiccup had been followed by quiet sobs. Ginny hurried the rest of the way to the table.

She twisted the cap off the bottle, breaking the seal, then set it on the table next to him as she eased herself into another chair. She wanted to take the child in her arms but knew that he might not be open to physical affection. Instead, she reached out tentatively and touched his shoulder. He didn't pull away, but his sobbing stopped. He lifted his head to lock eyes with hers, and she saw the tracks of tears on his skin.

"It's okay to cry," she said. "You've had a scary day. Mac and I are going to keep you safe. But it's still okay to cry."

He dragged the sleeve of his superhero sweatshirt across his eyes. Then he swiveled suddenly in the chair and launched himself at her, throwing his arms around her and burying his face in her shoulder. Once again, the soft sobbing started, heartbreakingly quiet in the big room.

Ginny rubbed his back as he cried. "That's right. Let it out. You're a good boy, Benji. We're so proud of you."

As she held the child and continued to rub his back, struck by how fragile he felt under her hand, she hoped that her promise to keep him safe was true. She knew she would do everything she could to make it true, but there were too many questions. Who were the men who'd shot up her cabin? Were they after her or after Mac? She wanted to believe Mac's security job had led to the situation they were in, but a part of her couldn't completely discard the possibility that the horrible hateful letters she'd received were merely the beginning of something much worse.

She knew she wasn't going to figure anything out by circling around the core questions again and again. For now, her top priority was to focus on the present and on keeping them alive until they could get somewhere safe. Still, the questions ate at her. She went through all her conversations with Willow over the last few weeks. She'd dismissed Willow's concerns more than once.

Because I always think I know better.

The guilt of that realization made her grip the child tighter, but that's when she realized he was no longer crying. At some point, Benji had fallen asleep, half standing and half cradled in her arms. She shifted on the chair to get a better grip and picked him up, making her sore muscles complain. Though she prided herself on being in shape, she didn't usually spend hours lugging small children through hilly forest terrain.

She carried Benji to the sofa and laid him down there, gently brushing the dark hair away from his small face. He was too young to have been through so much, though she'd helped children who were even younger than Benji, children who had seen even greater horrors. Benji was in pain, but he was still functional, which was helpful. She and Mac might need him to handle still more before they were out of danger.

Ginny realized she was stroking the child's head and moved her hand. The world could be so cruel. "But it can also be wonderful," she whispered. "Give it time. You're going to make it."

Though she should go to the kitchen and stir her pot of soup, Ginny sank down to sit on the coffee table beside the sofa. Exhaustion tugged at the edge of her awareness. She considered moving to one of the overstuffed leather chairs near the sofa and allowing herself a small nap. Even a short snooze could help her be sharper. Maybe it would be worth the risk.

She didn't move toward the kitchen or the chair but merely sat on the coffee table, hunched over with her forearms resting on her thighs while she drowsily debated in her head—stir the soup or take a nap? The two options had become almost a drone when the sound of a gunshot in the distance brought her instantly to her feet.

Mac!

7

At the sound of the gunshot, Mac threw himself against the rough wood siding of the outbuilding. The shooter wasn't close, but Mac knew how far a bullet could travel and how far a sniper could see with a scope. He pressed himself against the wood and listened.

Mac judged that the shot had come from the general direction of Ginny's cabin. Perhaps the shooter was disabling Mac's SUV. Another shot rang out. With his full attention on the sound, he was even more certain of the direction and the distance. Whatever the gunman fired at, it wasn't his little party of three.

Mac shifted position to better see the cabin. He worried that the gunshots would panic Ginny or Benji. Then he smiled. *Well, not Ginny.* He doubted the psychologist would be panicked by much of anything. She'd handled gunmen shooting up her vacation cabin coolly enough.

He trotted across the open space of the gravel drive, staying low. When he pulled open the cabin door to slip inside, his heart jumped in his chest. Ginny stood in the cabin's main room, aiming a shotgun at the door. Mac was no coward, but he felt the jolt at the sight of double barrels pointing at his chest.

Ginny lowered the gun immediately, and Mac took the opportunity to close the door behind him. "Who's shooting?" she whispered. "Do we need to move again?"

Mac shook his head. "It's not close. As best I can tell, it's coming from the direction of your cabin. I think the gunmen are disabling the SUV."

"That would make sense," she said. "So they're not shooting at us here."

"I don't see how." He gestured toward the shotgun. "Where did you get that? And where's Benji?" He scanned the room and spotted his nephew sleeping on the sofa.

"It's been a lot for him," Ginny said. She was still holding the shotgun, her handling of the weapon suggesting a familiarity with firearms that shouldn't have surprised him by that point. "He had a good cry and wore himself out. I decided to let him sleep until I knew what was going on, or until the food is ready."

Mac pointed. "And the shotgun?"

"It's Alan's. The lawyer who owns this cabin. He's scared to death of bears, though I suspect he'd be more danger to himself than the wildlife with this. He's not the outdoorsman he thinks he is."

Her casual familiarity with the owner of the cabin bothered Mac, and he realized that what he actually felt was jealousy. *That's ridiculous.* Pushing the thought aside, Mac focused on the aroma of something cooking. His stomach growled loudly. "Will the food be ready soon?"

"Should be," she said. "It's mostly canned vegetables, so it'll be best if it has a chance to simmer a few more minutes. At least Alan has a decent spice rack. Still, I wouldn't expect too much from the soup. Should be better than nothing though."

Hearing her say Alan's name bugged him again, and he shoved the jealousy down. "It smells good." He wasn't going to say anything else. He wasn't going to comment on her casual use of the cabin owner's name, but despite his plan, he heard himself say, "Alan?"

"Alan Forman," she said. "He's with a law firm in New York." The second detail was added with the slightest hint of annoyance, as if she thought Mac was wasting her time with the question.

"Right."

She stared at him, her expression unreadable. "If you're in need of a lawyer, I don't think Alan will be much help. He specializes in intellectual property law."

"I don't know what that is," Mac said, but he didn't actually care either, so he didn't mind when Ginny didn't bother to explain. He drifted in the direction of the kitchen, the smell of the cooking soup drawing him almost against his will. He was hungry. That had to be why he was acting so weird. It was hunger with a solid dose of fatigue added in.

When he got to the kitchen, he spotted a broken cracker on the counter and quickly ate it.

"How stale was that?" she asked. She carried the shotgun into the kitchen and laid it carefully on the counter well away from the camp stove.

"It was fine," he said. "I've reached the point where nearly anything would be fine."

"I know what you mean."

They studied one another for a long moment, neither revealing much by their expressions. Mac often used silence to get information from people when he needed it. He knew humans tended to fill any awkward silence, so he'd trained himself to be unbothered by it. It was becoming clear that Ginny had a similar tendency.

To his surprise, he felt the need to speak in order to end Ginny's quiet appraisal. It was unlike anything he'd encountered from another human before. Something in her dark-green eyes seemed to open his soul as easily as a book for casual perusal.

Unfortunately, all he could come up with was, "Is Benji going to be okay?" He knew the answer to that question was complicated.

Ginny paused, as if weighing her answer, then finally said, "Nothing about this is good for him, obviously, but he's a strong kid. With support and time, I think he's going to be fine."

"That's good."

Ginny walked over to pick up the pad Benji had been drawing on, then handed it to Mac. The top page showed a monster's head and chest. It had three eyes, two round blank ones on its head and a gaping one on its chest. It was the figure Benji always drew.

"You still have no idea who this figure could be?" Ginny asked him. He shook his head.

"Benji indicated that it wasn't either of his parents, or you."

"I could have told you that," Mac said dismissively.

"You could have, but it counts for more when Benji tells me." She folded her arms over her chest. "I think Benji's refusal to speak could be connected to the 'scary man' in his drawings. I can't know for certain without hearing from Benji himself, but I believe he may think the scary man wants him to keep quiet for some reason."

That got Mac's full attention. "You think someone is threatening him?"

"Not necessarily. The scary man might not even be real. It's possible that he represents Benji's fears in monster form."

"That's a lot to conclude from a kid's drawing."

"When I asked Benji specific questions about the drawing, he became agitated. I think it's somehow important for him to stay quiet. Again, that could be him trying to avoid the fears that plague him."

Mac frowned at the troublesome drawing. "It looks like a monster to me."

"Whatever is scaring Benji so much looks like a monster to him too."

———♡———

Though she watched Mac's face closely as they discussed Benji's drawing, it was clear he didn't know any more about it than he'd shared with her. She had become good at detecting lies over the years, and

Mac wasn't concealing information about his nephew. She was certain that his concern for Benji was real and untainted by any desire to keep something hidden about himself.

When Benji had held his finger over his lips to symbolize keeping quiet, the gesture had made her uneasy. It was so specific—maybe something a real person had done in front of him, which had obviously scared him. Given that, it wasn't unreasonable to imagine Mac could be the man in the drawing. Benji could have split his experience into real and unreal, shoving Mac's dangerous side into the invented monster. But that would mean Mac was lying now, and she'd stake her reputation on her confidence that he was not.

"How often does Benji create this drawing?" she asked.

"I'm not sure," Mac said. He set the paper on the table. "He's done it a bunch of times, but I haven't counted. I can see that it's creepy, but I assumed it was something from his nightmares about the crash." He shrugged. "All kids' drawings are pretty strange, right?"

"Sometimes," she agreed. "But the drawings of traumatized children, especially drawings they repeat, can hold clues to deeper meaning. It's a way of revisiting the trauma by transforming it into images the child can relate to, like scribbled monsters."

"What clues do you see there?" Mac asked, waving vaguely toward the sketch.

"I'm still working that out." She mentally set aside that problem in favor of something she could address at present. "I think the soup is ready. I'll make a bowl for Benji, but we should probably let it cool a little first before we wake him. It'll be too hot for him to eat right away."

"Can I have mine?" Mac asked.

"I thought we'd both go ahead and eat." She ladled out a bowl of soup for Benji and left it on the counter. Then she filled larger bowls for herself and Mac, which she carried to the table. "Will you grab the crackers?"

Mac did, and they sat down. Ginny pushed Benji's drawings aside. The soup was far from the most impressive meal Ginny had ever made, but it was hot and filling. They'd burned up a lot of calories during the day, so the sustenance helped her feel more human again and less desperate for a place to curl into a ball and sleep.

The second Mac finished his food, he asked, "Why do you have an escape tunnel in your cabin?"

Ginny hated talking about anything to do with her family, but considering what they'd been through, she didn't think it was the time for secrets. Besides, Mac had earned some trust. He'd more than done his part in keeping them alive. "My father was a paranoid survivalist. My mother inherited a sizeable sum from her parents, which my dad invested in a survivalist's dream home. Then he left an impressive job in finance to drag Mom and me up here."

"How old were you?" Mac asked.

"A little younger than Benji." She set her spoon into her bowl, no longer interested in finishing the last of the soup despite knowing she should. "My father wasn't cruel to my mother and me—not intentionally anyway. But he was driven by a fear that some unnamed threat was out to get us. So every day was full of drills and study on how to survive the horror he was certain loomed right in front of us."

"Sounds rough."

She shrugged. "I left when I was a teenager and walked all the way down the mountain. I became an emancipated minor and managed to put myself through college, with help from scholarships and grants. I never reconnected with my parents. I never even tried."

Mac whistled. "And they didn't search for you?"

"Apparently not." She rose and picked up the bowls. "I didn't even know when they died until I received a letter from the lawyer. My father had left me the property. I didn't do anything with it for years, but then I decided I could remodel the house and try to erase the past." Her lips twisted wryly. "With mixed results."

"We're lucky you didn't erase all of it."

"The irony of my paranoid father being right in this case hasn't escaped me." Ginny was surprised at how much easier it had been to talk about her past than she'd expected. She rarely spoke of her parents to anyone, and then only when absolutely necessary. It felt good to share it with someone. But she knew that the relief she felt could build a false sense of connection with the man. He was still a stranger. And she was better off on her own, so she forced her emotional shield up, telling herself that she hadn't even noticed his kind eyes.

"I think it's time Benji had some dinner," she said.

"You're probably right," Mac said. He stood and stepped in front of Ginny. "You've been amazing all day, but don't feel like you have to carry everything on your own. We're not out of this yet. And our chances of survival increase if we stick together."

Ginny gave him a single quick nod, then eased around him to gently wake Benji. "Come on, buddy. Supper's ready."

The little boy was surprisingly enthusiastic about the soup and spooned it rapidly into his mouth after Ginny got him seated at the table and gave him the cooled bowl. He also ate several of the slightly stale crackers while swinging his legs under the table. Ginny was glad to see how refreshed he was. As Mac had said, they still had a lot ahead of them.

"Ginny," Mac said. "What do you know about that shed in the yard? What's in it?"

"Alan has an ATV. I heard him use it once. It makes a ridiculous amount of noise, and I was worried he'd be tearing through the woods with the thing, but he never did. Maybe he found it as obnoxious as I did, or at least not as much fun as he'd hoped."

"It sounds as if you know him well."

She gave a small chuckle. "Not really. My judgment of Alan was that he often invested in things he hoped would be fun but that ultimately disappointed him. He once told me he was trying to sell a yacht. When I asked him why, he said he never could get over the seasickness."

"Is there anything in the shed other than the ATV?" Mac asked.

"Not that I know of," she said. "He probably has an axe since he has a fireplace, so he might have that and some other tools in the shed, but I'm not sure. Honestly, I've never been in there."

"An ATV wouldn't be a great escape vehicle for three people with gunmen in the area. As you noted, they're noisy, and they don't offer much protection from flying bullets."

"We have another option," Ginny said. Mac raised his eyebrows, and she continued. "Alan's cabin is on the last piece of private land before we hit a state park. At the top of this hill, there's a ranger station."

"Hill?" Mac echoed. "I'd call it a mountain."

"Maybe a small one," she conceded. "Getting to the top involves a hike of several miles, and some of it is seriously rough going, but there's always a ranger on duty up there. They'd have vehicles and reliable communication."

"You think we can make it to the station with a child?" Mac asked.

"I do. Benji can walk, and I know of one other place we can rest along the way if we need to."

"We should get going as soon as night falls," Mac said. "If we make the climb in the dark, we'll be less likely to get shot."

"Maybe, but there are other risks."

"Such as?"

"We won't be able to be as quiet in the dark. And this area is home to bobcats, coyotes, and bears. The chance of running into one of those is greater in the dark since they tend to be more active at night to avoid humans."

"Good thing we have a shotgun then."

She smiled dryly. "A shotgun with exactly two shells—the two Alan was stupid enough to leave in. The man is lucky he didn't suffer a horrible accident with a loaded weapon leaning in the corner of his bedroom. At any rate, I couldn't find any other ammunition for it."

"Maybe we should search harder," Mac said. "There must be some."

"Maybe," she said. But she was far from certain. It wouldn't have shocked her if the two shells were truly all that was in the cabin. Alan was not a hunter, or any kind of outdoorsman, really. He kept the gun because he was afraid of bears, not so he could shoot regularly.

"I'll hunt for more ammunition while Benji finishes eating," Mac said. "Then we should pack up and get moving. It's not fully dark, but it's getting there."

She hated the thought of wandering through the woods at night. Her father would have called her a fool for considering it. But Mac had a point. In the dark, they'd be much harder to find, assuming the men coming after them didn't have night vision tools of some kind. And her father had drilled her on finding her way in the woods blindfolded, so she knew she could lead the way.

All they had to do was avoid bears and murderers. How hard could it be?

8

While she repacked her duffel, Ginny fought a wave of irritation at Mac for insisting they take Benji out in the woods in the dark. She'd grown up in the area. He must realize she knew the risks better than he did. They'd be safer if they waited until light.

But even as she stuffed items in her bag, she could see that her thinking was flawed. Staying in Alan's cabin wasn't safe. The windows were large, and it would be a lot harder to avoid weapon fire given so much visibility through the glass. And there was no reason to assume the gunmen wouldn't find the place eventually.

Ginny slowed her movements, taking deep breaths to restore her calm. She needed to be smart, especially with what she packed. If she made the bag too heavy, she risked slowing them down. If she left something out, it could end up being the one thing that would have saved them.

It would help if they had more weapons. Scanning the kitchen idly, she spotted Alan's pepper grinder, and an idea was born. She tore a paper towel off the nearby roll and ground pepper into it. Once she had a good pile, she folded up the napkin and tucked it into her pocket.

She mulled over her problem with Mac. As much as she didn't care to admit it, she knew part of her irritation was simply the fact that she didn't appreciate being told what to do. But she could see the wisdom of Mac's idea. If it were merely the two of them, it would have been the suggestion she made herself. She could move through the woods in the dark without issue, even as bone-weary as she already felt. But Benji was an added vulnerability.

At least he'd had a short nap. As if her thoughts had summoned him, Benji appeared at her side and held up the notepad.

"You want to bring this?" she asked. He nodded, so she added it to the bag without argument. The kid asked for little enough. "You should rest until we have to go. It won't be long."

He walked obediently to the sofa, but he didn't lie down. Instead, his eyes were on the windows. Though mostly covered by thick drapes, they did offer a shaft of light from a gap between the curtains. Ginny could tell that light was much dimmer than it had been when they arrived. The interior of the cabin had become deeply shadowed as time passed.

When she'd been searching Alan's cupboards earlier, she'd found a thermos. Moving to the kitchen, she used the last of the fuel in the camp stove to make coffee and filled the container. She and Mac would need the boost from the caffeine later. The flame sputtered out on the stove, and she wished she had extra cans of fuel, but since she didn't, she'd simply leave the camp stove behind and save the weight.

She emptied another find from the cupboard—a box of cereal bars—into her bag, figuring Benji would find them more palatable than the protein bars she already had in there. The protein bars were an excellent source of energy, but the taste was astonishingly disgusting.

Mac's footsteps announced his approach even before he stepped into view. She didn't take her eyes off her packing, but in her peripheral vision she noted frustration in the way he ran a hand through his dark hair. "I couldn't find any more ammunition. Are you sure he didn't store any in here?"

"I opened every drawer, cupboard, and canister when we arrived," she said. "There are no shotgun shells."

"Then we'll have to make these two count," he said.

"What about your handgun?"

Again, his fingers passed through his hair. "It's out. I wasn't on a job, so I didn't prepare for a gunfight."

"I didn't mean for that to sound judgmental. I'd be more concerned if you spent your days armed to the teeth, especially with a child around."

Ginny zipped the bag closed, then peered across the gloomy room toward Benji. The mountain would get cold after dark. Benji's sweatshirt would help, but it wasn't enough. "Hold on."

She headed into the cabin's lone bedroom. The windows in it were smaller, and the drapes did a better job of blocking the light. The room was almost completely dark. She crossed to the dresser and opened a drawer, feeling around for the contents. She found something soft and wooly—a sweater, and from the feel of it, an expensive one. "I'll get you a new one," she promised her neighbor under her breath as she pulled the sweater out of the drawer. She quickly located a couple more and carried the garments into the great room.

"You'll need another sweater, Benji," she said. "It's going to be chillier outside than it was earlier."

Benji faced her, but his features were indistinct in the shadows. She pulled the sweater over his head. It would be long, nearly to the boy's knees, but that would make it even warmer. The sleeves were a problem though. She could roll them up, but they'd still fall over the boy's hands again and again. "Hold on," she said.

She could see Mac standing near her bag but could not read his expression any more than she had Benji's. She stepped around him, shoved the other sweaters into the duffel, and grabbed a pair of kitchen shears from Alan's knife block.

She carried the shears over to Benji and cut off the excess sleeve length, wincing slightly as she again felt the soft, expensive fabric.

Desperate times. She renewed her mental promise to replace the clothes she'd taken.

"We should be ready to go," she called to Mac. "Let me get the bag."

"I've got it."

Ginny tensed. She really didn't want to let the bag out of her own hands. It was the most important thing they carried. "You should carry the gun," she said. "I can carry the bag."

"It's heavy," Mac said. "And it won't do to wear you out when we need you so much."

"It's okay. I'm stronger than my size would suggest."

"And more stubborn," he replied. "But this time I insist. I can carry the bag and the shotgun. You hold Benji's hand. Do you think we can risk a light?"

"I found another flashlight in the kitchen," she said. "But even if we shield the beam, it's going to be risky. We don't need to give the shooters something to aim at. We'll have it if we need it, but otherwise, we should try to rely on moonlight as much as possible."

"Sounds reasonable."

Benji's hand slipped into hers, and she squeezed it. "I'm sorry we have to walk some more, but I'm not sure it would be safe to stay here any longer. You're doing great."

The front door opened, and Ginny saw Mac step out, his head swiveling as he searched the area. She knew it was probably darker in the cabin than it was outside, but she still doubted he could see far. He gestured for them to follow him, so Ginny squeezed Benji's hand again, and together they stepped out into the gloaming.

———♡———

Though he'd considered carrying Benji, Mac had decided against it. The boy was doing fine on his own. Mac knew that even a short nap could make a big difference in a survival situation. He thought of the times he'd done security details with Derrick, and they'd taken turns napping to help them stay sharp. Derrick had woken after each snooze with the clearheaded high energy of a natural morning person. It appeared his son was the same way. Good thing, since Mac tended to wake groggy and grumpy.

They crossed the lawyer's yard quickly and quietly and soon reached the woods. Mac shifted the duffel higher on his shoulder, wincing. The bag was heavier than he'd expected, causing him to marvel at Ginny as she slipped through the trees. She'd appeared to carry it so easily through the tunnel.

His security company employed a few women who were strong, fast, and tough, so it wasn't as if strong women were new to him. And in light of Ginny's history, nothing about her should have been surprising. Ginny had been raised by survivalists. Luckily for him and his nephew, she hadn't completely given up the drive to be ready for anything.

As they slipped through the woods, Ginny and Benji moved into the lead, which made sense. She knew the area. With no track or trail, her memory was all they had for a map. The moon wasn't full, but it still offered more visibility than Mac had expected.

Mac suspected he was a liability in their situation. He was a city kid, urban to the bone. He had rarely experienced complete darkness. The moonlight left enough pools of shadow in the woods to make Mac jumpy. When he'd been a kid, he'd read an adventure story about a wolf tracking a man through dark woods. The story had given him nightmares for weeks, and at the moment he felt as if he'd stepped right into it. He wished Ginny hadn't mentioned the animals in the forest.

He shook off the old story and focused intently on the woman in front of him. She moved through the trees as if the darkness didn't bother her at all, and he suspected that she'd be even faster if she weren't trying to conserve Benji's strength.

Several times they had to skirt around fallen branches, but nothing disoriented Ginny. Every movement she made radiated with purpose. She stopped suddenly, and Mac was instantly on alert. Had she spotted something? He scanned the area. She stepped closer to him and tapped his chest, then pointed. He followed the gesture and saw a bright white blaze painted on a tree.

She leaned close and whispered, "That marks the trail to the station."

He nodded, glad of proof that they were on the right track.

They continued up. In the dark, it was impossible not to step on the occasional stick, and each time one of them did so, Mac's skin crawled as he imagined one of the gunmen hearing the sound and realizing where they were. Even more frightening than his own snapping sticks was when he heard brush breaking and loud rustling in the distance. Mac peered in the direction of the noise every time, but nothing but darkness and shadow met his eyes.

The trail was steep, but walking was still considerably easier on the open ground. Moonlight slipped through the trees more easily along the trail. With a clear path ahead, Mac was less enthusiastic about Ginny and Benji leading. He could see they were both beginning to lag as well, so he picked up speed to catch up and lay a hand on Ginny's shoulder.

She stopped and Benji immediately leaned against her side.

"Let me lead."

She dipped her head and eased to the side to let Mac pass. He took care not to hurry, though he was so tired that rushing up the side of a mountain was impossible, even if he did want to reach the ranger station as soon as they could. He heard more noises around them, some soft, some louder. He suspected that if he knew what caused each one, he wouldn't find the knowledge particularly comforting.

It took a concerted effort to put one foot in front of the other, each step feeling as if he were shifting a load many times his weight. Ginny's bag grew heavier and heavier, and more than once Mac was tempted to hand it off to her again. But he quickly suppressed the urge.

He was entertaining the thought of unloading the bag into a bush when a man stepped out onto the trail in front of Mac and leveled a gun at him. It happened so fast, and Mac was so tired, that he had no time to raise the shotgun in response.

"Drop the weapon," the man said. "Or I'll shoot the woman. And you." The man raised his voice to carry in the darkness. "Don't try running, or I'll shoot you all."

Mac recognized the face of the gunman who'd been watching the tunnel end. It was clear he and his partner had grown tired of waiting for them and decided on a more direct assault. Mac set the shotgun down. He almost expected the man to simply open fire. After all, that was what they'd done at Ginny's cabin. Why change tactics now?

Then Mac realized the plan probably hadn't changed. The shooter simply wanted to be sure to kill all of them.

"Come on up here," the man said. "Come stand beside this guy. Bring the boy."

Mac heard the sound of movement behind him. Don't, he thought, wishing desperately that he could shove his thoughts into Ginny's head. Run. Get Benji out of here.

"What are you doing?" the man bellowed. "Get the kid up here."

"He fell," Ginny answered, her voice quavering. She sounded near tears. "He's worn out."

"He'll be worse than worn out if you don't get up here," the man snarled.

"I'm coming, I'm coming," Ginny said, her voice thick with dread.

Mac considered rushing the man. He'd be shot, but maybe he could hold the man long enough for Ginny and Benji to dive off the trail.

Mac heard crashing in the trees nearby. "Is that your partner?" he asked.

"Probably," the man said. "Now get that kid up here."

Ginny sobbed in response. Mac suspected the sudden crying was some kind of act and Ginny had concocted a plan, but since he couldn't guess what that plan might be, he wasn't able to do anything to help.

Still, he could try. "Can't you see she's doing the best she can?" he demanded.

"Do better!"

The crashing got louder and was joined by a growl that bordered on a roar.

It was not the other gunman.

Mac jumped away, unconcerned about the gun in the other man's hand. He need not have worried. The gunman had a much bigger problem.

A large black bear crashed through the brush and onto the trail ahead of the gunman. The bear grunted and wheezed as it galloped toward him like a train picking up speed on a hill. The gunman yelled, his full attention on the bear.

Mac heard movement behind him and knew Ginny was getting Benji off the trail while the distraction offered the opportunity. Mac snatched the shotgun from the ground and dove off the trail after Ginny and Benji, quickly putting a tree between himself and the gunman. He knew they needed to get out of there, but the shock of seeing a bear explode out of the woods had temporarily dulled his reflexes. He'd dealt with all sorts of dangerous humans in his job, but he was a city guy. He'd never seen a bear outside of a zoo. He thought of what little he knew about the animals. Hadn't he read that one should never run from a bear? He certainly felt like running, but maybe he should stay behind and fight the bear to keep it from chasing Ginny and Benji. That way they could escape. He peeked around the tree.

The sight of a massive bear rushing toward him had temporarily frozen the shooter, but he rallied a split second before the bear would hit him. He fired a shot, but it missed the huge creature, who was on the man in seconds, snarling and plowing him down with its sheer bulk. The man screamed, but Mac couldn't tell what was going on. In the dark, the bear barely appeared to move at all.

Mac felt the leather of his jacket bunch on his arm as someone grabbed him. Ginny's expression reflected none of the shock he felt. They were in her environment, every bit as much as the college auditorium had been. "We need to go while the bear is distracted," she said, no trace of tears in her voice now.

"I thought you weren't supposed to run from bears."

"Trust me."

So he did. And the sound of shouts and growls behind kept him moving, burning off his weariness, at least for the moment. It would have to be enough.

More and more he was beginning to realize that the moment was all they had.

9

Climbing the mountain toward the ranger station was no longer an option, and Ginny knew it. Thankfully, she'd remembered another option. Even in the darkness, she knew exactly where they were from the position of the moon and the steepness of the trail. It had been years, but the lessons drilled into her had barely faded.

Climbing higher wasn't a choice. They weren't fast enough with a tired child in tow. Even if one of the two gunmen had been slowed down by the bear, the other was in the woods somewhere. They needed to reach a place that would be safe and hard to find, and she knew exactly the spot.

As she slipped through the trees holding Benji's hand, she oriented herself by the position of the moon, as well as landmarks that wouldn't have moved over the years, such as the outcropping of rock up ahead that had reminded her of a castle ruin when she was a young, imaginative child. As they skirted the rock, Benji stumbled, but Ginny managed to catch him before he could fall against the sharp stone.

Mac appeared beside them. He scooped up the child, and Benji automatically wrapped himself around his uncle. Mac passed the duffel to Ginny without comment. She shouldered the weight without protest because it would have done no good to complain. Mac wasn't a pack mule.

As they left the rock outcropping behind them, Ginny thought of all the men she'd met since leaving her parents. There had been a few who'd been certain they knew everything of value, never even considering the possibility that Ginny might know more or be a better judge of what they should do. She accepted that men were often conditioned from the time they were children to see themselves as strong leaders, and it was hard to hand that over to someone they thought should be following orders rather than giving them. Mac had put his trust in her as they trudged through the darkness, and that was a rarity in her experience.

She had been walking as quickly as she dared, but a part of her attention was constantly alert for sounds around them. She should never have been surprised on the path by the gunman. They'd been lucky, but she couldn't count on luck keeping them alive.

So far, she'd heard nothing she couldn't identify. If her memory was accurate, they should be nearly ready to rest.

The terrain had grown steeper, as she'd remembered. They'd circled around to the other, rougher side of the mountain, changing elevation slightly. Her eyes swept the increasingly rocky surroundings, and she experienced an instant of panic, certain she should have found her destination already. Had she gotten lost?

Then she saw it—a jagged darkness in the side of a boulder. The boulder was cracked, that much was obvious, but what most passersby wouldn't see was the fact that the crack gave access to a cave where the same water that split the boulder had hollowed out part of the mountain.

Ginny had spent hours in the cave as a child and even into her early teens. It would be plenty big enough inside, but getting in was going to be a challenge for a man as big as Mac. It was why heading to the cave hadn't been a priority before. But with their alternatives dwindling, they would have to find a way. He'd gotten out of the broken pipe tunnel when it looked as if he wouldn't fit. He'd simply have to get into the cave as well.

Ginny pulled Alan's flashlight from her pocket and pushed the end into the crack before switching it on. She swept it around as much as she dared, listening for the rustling of creatures inside.

"What is that?" Mac asked, his voice so close she felt his breath.

"A cave. It's big inside."

Mac eased passed her and thrust an arm into the crack, then pulled it out. "It'll be tight."

"You think you can make it?"

"Sure," he said, though he didn't sound as confident as she would have liked.

"I'll go first and make sure there are no animals inside." She set the bag on the ground and slipped through the crack. It was easier than she remembered, and she realized time and wear had widened the space a little, which was incredibly fortunate. It could just as easily have shifted the boulder, pushing the crack closed. She felt a wave of gratitude that one thing had gone their way.

The passage through the opening was short, and she soon found herself inside the spacious cavern. She could stand easily. She waved her flashlight around. Though there were signs that animals had been there, including the shed skin of a snake, there was nothing alive in there anymore.

Ginny thrust her arm through the crack. "It's fine. Pass me the bag."

She soon felt the bulk of the duffel pressed against her hand. She dragged it through the crack and set it to one side. "Now Benji."

Benji was through the gap in seconds, though he stumbled at the last step and she had to catch him. The child was beyond exhausted. "We're going to rest now," she told him, then called through the gap. "Benji is in."

"Good. I'm going to do a quick scout around, then I'll join you."

"Okay." Ginny had kept her arm around Benji during the exchange, worried that the boy would stagger into something and fall. She gave him her full attention. "I think there's a good spot to sit over here." She led the boy to a fairly smooth, flat spot, then put a hand on his shoulder. "Hold on one second."

She pulled a folded sheet of thick plastic from her bag and spread it out, knowing the rock would be cold and probably damp. She hoped the plastic would help with the dampness at any rate. Then she found the extra sweater she'd gotten from Alan's drawer and laid it on the plastic sheet. Finally, she added a shiny emergency blanket. She wrapped the blanket around the child and settled him on the sweater. He curled up as much as he could and closed his eyes.

Ginny wished she could have done more to make the child comfortable. If they weren't being chased by gunmen, she could have made him a decent bed out of pine branches, but she could see that the boy's exhaustion had done what her store of supplies couldn't. He was asleep within a few breaths.

Ginny pulled another folded plastic square from her bag and spread it on the floor of the cave before sitting down. She had chosen a spot out of direct line of sight of the crack, so she found another glow stick and cracked it. The light wasn't bright, but it was enough. She switched off the flashlight and waited for Mac, trying not to worry about the fact that he hadn't yet returned.

The area around the cave was steep enough to be treacherous. As they'd stumbled through the trees, Mac had wished for easier passage until he'd remembered that what was hard for them would be hard for their pursuers as well. Ideally, the gunmen wouldn't be as familiar with the area as Ginny was, which would give the three of them another advantage. He was glad the cave entrance was nearly invisible, though he wished he had enough light to tell if they'd left signs of their passage. *Though if I can't see it, maybe they can't either.*

He followed the sound of water to a small creek that ran down a nearby hill, thinking it would be handy in the morning. Mac knew he was putting off shoving himself into that narrow crack. He wasn't a fan of tight spaces. The tunnel exit had been bad enough, but the crack in the rock was even more alarming.

Then again, my crashing around out here is only increasing the possibility that we're going to be found. Mac knew that *crashing* wasn't exactly the right word. His movements were fairly quiet for an exhausted man in the dark. But he should still buck up and get into the cave.

He had barely reached the crack in the boulder when he heard exactly the kind of crashing he'd accused himself of coming from the woods. He stopped and raised the shotgun with painful slowness, hoping desperately that the sound was a deer and not a man. He aimed the gun toward the sound, hoping he wouldn't have to pull the trigger. He'd do whatever he had to do, but he didn't want to kill someone if he could avoid it.

What broke through the brush was neither a man nor deer. It was the bear they'd encountered on the trail, the one that had inadvertently saved them from the gunman. Mac had no doubt it was the same animal.

Mac slowly edged toward the crack in the rock. With the bulk of the creature, Mac doubted the bear would fit through the crack. At least, he hoped it wouldn't. Even if it did, he'd have the upper hand if the bear tried to squeeze through the gap. All Mac had to do was get inside.

He couldn't let himself think of what would happen if he couldn't get through.

He kept the shotgun trained on the bear. He could shoot the creature, but that would bring the gunmen down on them. If he fired the weapon, they'd have to clear out and move fast. He wasn't sure any of them were fit to do that.

Cross that bridge if you come to it, his mind screamed. Still, he couldn't quite decide what to do. As soon as he began squeezing into the crack, shooting wouldn't be an option. And if the bear got in, it might very well kill him right in front of Ginny and Benji, then move on to them.

He couldn't risk it. He stepped away from the cracked boulder, keeping the gun focused on the bear and weighing the possibility of using the shotgun as a cudgel to avoid alerting the other killers in the woods. The bear took a step toward him, growling.

Suddenly, something bounced out of the crack in the rock and landed near the bear's front paws. It jerked away. Another thing landed beside the first. The bear lowered its huge head and sniffed. It was wounded and angry, but a bear was a bear. And the first thing on any bear's mind was his stomach. The massive animal gobbled up the sweet-smelling cereal bars at its feet.

Something yanked at Mac's sleeve. "Come on!" Ginny hissed fiercely.

Mac spared her a glance. He wasn't sure about the logic of trapping themselves inside the cave, especially since she'd proven they had something tempting to eat.

"Mac, move!"

Ultimately the decision was simple. Staying outside of the cave wasn't an option. Another cereal bar flew across the clearing, landing past the bear and forcing the creature to move away to reach it. Then Ginny disappeared into the crack in the boulder. Once again, Mac chose to trust the woman he'd known for such a short time and shoved himself into the hole.

His quick movement must have caught the bear's notice. Mac heard the bear's growl and knew it no longer cared about cereal bars. Even as Mac shoved himself deeper into the tight crack, he heard the thudding of heavy paws on the ground outside.

The bear was coming.

Mac pushed harder. The rocks dug into him at a dozen different spots, all promising bruises—or worse.

Pain flamed. The bear had managed to rake its claws down his arm. The leather jacket deflected some of the damage, but he could feel that it hadn't protected him from all of it.

Mac would have sworn he had no more adrenaline left after everything they'd been through, but the bite of bear claws into his forearm proved him wrong. A surge of strength drove him through the rest of the tight crack. He felt his clothes tearing and blood trickling from rock scrapes on his face and the bear's scratch on his arm, but none of the pain slowed him down. He had one hope, and he continued to push himself toward it.

With a final effort, he popped through. He staggered into the larger cavern, and Ginny's arm circled him, hauling him away from the crack in the wall faster than he could have managed on his own. She pushed him against the wall and tugged the shotgun out of his hand.

"Don't shoot," he said, his voice sounding far away. "Too loud."

She didn't bother to answer, and Mac leaned against the wall. He saw Benji asleep on the other side of the cavern and realized that meant there was a light. It was a creepy green, and it took longer than it should for him to realize it was another chemical glow stick.

Mac raised his arm to check the severity of his injuries. He couldn't tell if it was the sight of his free-flowing blood or simply the compounding of everything he'd been through, but the cave tilted and his knees gave out. He collapsed to the floor of the cavern.

10

Ginny was too far away to stop Mac's fall, though she sprinted to his side in time to slow his descent. He still hit the rock floor, but not hard. It was more of a slow crumple.

"Are you hurt?"

"Not too bad."

Ginny had to take that at face value as she didn't have time for discussion. She heard the bear grunting and growling as it tried to force itself into the cave. Grabbing the glow stick from the floor, she moved to the crack in the cave wall. The light let her see the bear. It wouldn't give up on getting in—not on its own—after she'd fed it to keep it from attacking Mac. She reached into her pocket and pulled out the packet of pepper. She unfolded it, took a deep breath, and blew the contents off the paper towel toward the bear with as much force as she could manage.

The bear's reaction was a dramatic retreat. It jerked free of the crack, gagging and sneezing. Ginny hated to hurt an animal, but she'd hate it more if the bear had made it into the cave and gone after Benji.

She waited. No more sound came from the crack in the boulder. The bear wanted nothing else to do with them.

Stuffing the paper towel into her blazer pocket, she crouched beside Mac. He hadn't stirred from the place he'd landed, which Ginny suspected was a bad sign. She lifted Mac's arm to search for wounds.

The rip in his jacket revealed scratches, likely from the bear. "I'm going to need to cut this sleeve away."

"No," Mac said. He shrugged out of his jacket with a grunt of pain.

In some ways, the bleeding was a good sign. It would help to flush out the wound, reducing the odds that he'd get an infection from the bear's claws.

"This isn't too bad," she said. "Not nearly as bad as it could have been, anyway. I'll clean and bandage it."

Mac leaned against the wall. "Have at it."

Ginny reached behind her and snagged the strap on her duffel to drag it toward her. She found the first aid kit easily and pulled it out. The box was old, but she'd chosen and packed the contents herself with a focus on serious injury, not the small stick-on bandages and antiseptic wipes of the usual kits.

She held one of their flashlights in her mouth as she worked, using it to light the wound area. The first aid kit included a squirt bottle of sterile saline, and she was able to clean the wound enough to examine it. The bear's claws had dug deeper than she'd hoped, but Mac's arm would still be usable.

Though she treated the wounds as gently as she could, Mac hissed several times. She found the sounds endearing in a strange way, proof that he was human and not simply the hulking, bossy pest she'd made him out to be. He'd done as much to keep them alive as she had, and she had no doubt that he'd give his life for the little boy sleeping on the other side of the cavern.

"What did you do to that bear?" Mac asked. "I thought it would come in here for sure."

She began wrapping his arm in sterile gauze. "I blew pepper in his face, and he lost interest."

Mac laughed aloud, then winced. "You are the most fascinating woman I've ever met."

"Nice to hear," she said. She tucked the end of the gauze into the wrap. "This should keep the wound clean. I think you'll heal okay without stitches, though I did close the deepest scratch with some butterfly bandages. Try not to overuse that arm if possible."

"That should be easy enough," he said dryly. "I'm sure the rest of our time in the woods will be smooth sailing."

"We need to stay here through the night," Ginny said firmly. "The men hunting us don't have that bear's nose. I don't believe we'll be found tonight. The woods are considerably more dangerous than this cave. We'll also be better tomorrow if we rest tonight."

"Sounds good," he said. "I wouldn't have found this place if you hadn't brought us here." He inclined his head in Benji's direction. "How is he doing?"

"Exhausted, but better than I could ever have guessed. Your nephew is extraordinary."

"Takes after his folks," Mac said. He rested his head against the wall of the cave. "We should keep a watch."

"I agree. And the one not on watch should sleep next to Benji, as close as possible. His small size makes him much more susceptible to the cold. I did the best I could to make him comfortable, but my go bag didn't include an inflatable mattress."

Mac grinned. "I'm surprised."

"I left it out so I'd have room for the dinghy."

His eyes widened. "You have a dinghy in there?"

Ginny laughed. "Of course not. But I do have some more emergency blankets. Go over and lie down next to Benji. I'll cover you both with another blanket."

Mac frowned. "No, I can take the first watch."

"Don't argue with me. You're injured. I'm not. The sleep you get now will make you much stronger tomorrow, and that's when we'll need you."

Mac's expression darkened, and Ginny braced for a serious argument, but he didn't say anything at all. Instead, he simply blew out a long, harsh breath. "I think you'll need to help me."

She did, hauling him up with considerable effort. No wonder he hadn't argued further. The man was practically dead on his feet. He leaned heavily on her as they crossed the room. "Wake me in four hours."

"No problem," she replied. *Especially since I'll do no such thing.*

Mac settled down next to Benji. He tucked his uninjured arm under his head and draped the other over the boy. Ginny covered him as much as possible with his jacket, then added another emergency blanket from her bag. She tucked the edges of the cover around them, noting that Mac had already fallen asleep.

She studied the big man and the small boy. They'd both been through a lot, and her heart went out to them. Each had been amazing in his own way. *Together we've been a team.*

She was surprised to find that she wanted them to stay that way. For the first time in her life, and even in their current situation, she preferred their presence to her own company. Standing over them in the silent cave, where Mac's breathing was the loudest thing she could hear, she closed her eyes and said a silent prayer for safety through the rest of the night.

Then she crossed again to her bag and pulled out the last of her emergency blankets. She shook it out and wrapped herself in it, then wedged herself in the crack. She could tell from her exhaustion that she wasn't fit to keep watch, but if anything tried to come in, she couldn't help but notice. Her father had taught her tricks to stay awake on watch, but she ignored them all and fell deeply asleep.

Mac woke with a start, aware of a dozen different aches of varying severity. He lifted his arm from Benji, and his nephew's eyes popped open. He looked at Mac and smiled. Mac's heart jumped in his chest. It was the first smile he'd gotten from the child since he'd taken him in. In that smile, Mac could see the laughing boy he'd known before. *And after spending the night in a cave, plus half of yesterday running for our lives.*

"Hi, kiddo," Mac said quietly. He rolled over and sat up. Ginny was across the cavern, rifling through the duffel. Her clothes were dirty and her hair had gone wild overnight, but he was stunned by how beautiful she was. He pushed the thought down viciously.

Mac struggled to his feet, every muscle in his body protesting the movement. It would be a while before the stiffness of a night on the ground worked itself out. He crossed the cavern, taking care not to limp. "You were supposed to wake me."

"I fell asleep," she said. He was shocked by the total lack of guilt or apology in her voice.

"Apparently we survived anyway," he said.

"Apparently." She gave him her full attention, her expression intent. "You okay? No throbbing in your arm? No fever?"

"I feel fine, other than the normal aches from sleeping on the ground." He flexed his arm tentatively. It hurt, but not so much that he couldn't ignore it. "I don't suppose we have any food?"

"Energy bars," she said, tossing one his way. From her sharp eyes, he knew the throw was a test, and he was glad he'd managed to catch it. "Don't judge by the taste. They're the best on the market. I had some cereal bars, which would have helped get the disgusting flavor out of our mouths, but the bear ate them. I have one left, but it's for Benji."

"Sounds fair."

Benji must have heard her too, as he held out a hand, and she dropped a strawberry cereal bar into it. Benji plopped down on the ground and peeled away the wrapper.

Ginny surprised Mac again by pulling a drink box out of the bag and stabbing a straw into it before holding it out to Benji as well. "Chocolate milk," she said. "Shelf stable. Alan had it in his cupboard."

"Do you have one of those in there for me?" Mac asked as he eased himself down to sit as well.

"No, but I have coffee." She pulled out the thermos she'd filled at the cabin. "It's not hot anymore, but it's warm, so we have to take our positives where we can." She poured some of the coffee into the cap of the thermos and handed it to Mac.

They fell silent as they ate. Mac did his best not to make faces at the flavor combination of gluey protein bar and bitter coffee. He couldn't be picky. They'd need all the energy they could get to stay alive.

"I'm not sure the ranger station is a safe choice anymore," Mac said.

"Why not?"

"We met that gunman on the trail to the station, which means they're probably aware of it. They could be waiting for us there."

"True," she agreed. "Any ideas?"

"I think I have to backtrack and grab your friend's ATV. I can go alone and get help. You two stay right here. No one is going to find you in this cave, and I can return with the authorities in a couple hours." Even as he said the words, Mac hated the plan. He didn't want to leave Benji and Ginny in danger, even if he did believe that bringing them with him would be even more dangerous.

"And you're confident you can make it alone?" she asked.

"It's safer on my own. I can move faster, and I can drive more recklessly, which I will need to do. There's no cover on the ATV, and the noise of starting it up will draw the shooters' attention. However, that's good too. Pulling them off the mountain means they'll be farther from you and Benji."

"I hate this idea," she said.

"I'm open to hearing a different one."

She pressed her lips together but offered no plan. His was all they had.

Mac decided to add the detail he knew she'd hate most of all. "You keep the shotgun."

"That makes no sense," Ginny said. "You'll be the one out there with the shooters."

"True, but I'd have to toss it once I got on the ATV anyway. It will do more good here with you."

Her expression made it clear she was deeply unhappy, but again she offered nothing to refute his idea.

Mac dusted off his hands. "Well, that breakfast was one of the worst I've ever had, but I'm sure it'll do me good. I should get going while it's early."

He shifted to rise, and Benji launched himself from the ground, wrapping his arms around his uncle's neck. Mac held still and returned the embrace. "You need to stay here with Ginny. It'll be all right."

He felt his nephew's face press against his neck, and the dampness suggested Benji was crying. "You'll be okay," Mac insisted.

"I don't think Benji is worried about himself," Ginny said. She rubbed the boy's thin shoulder. "I know you want to be with Mac, but we need you here, Benji."

The boy clung to his uncle even harder. Mac understood. Adults had told Benji a lot of stupid things since his parents had died, starting with "it's going to be okay."

"It's true," she assured him.

Benji let Mac set him down. Mac knelt to address the kid directly. "We'd stick together if it was the best way to handle things, but I don't think it is. We have to be smart and brave. I know you're both." He squeezed the boy's shoulders. "I love you, Benji."

Benji hugged him again desperately. Mac let the boy hold on for as long as he needed. Finally, Benji took a step away, moving closer to Ginny. Mac met her eyes. "Take care of my favorite nephew."

"I will. And he'll take care of me."

With a pain that felt as if he were leaving part of himself behind, Mac stepped into the crack to get going on what was probably the worst plan he'd ever made. He didn't have a lot of hope. The combination of meeting the shooter on the trail and being attacked by a bear the night before hadn't left him feeling all that impressed by his own abilities.

Without Ginny's knowledge of the woods, Mac had to rely on backtracking the route they'd taken the day before as well as he could. He felt the lack of a weapon severely. At one point, he picked up a sharp-edged rock and shoved it into his pocket. Farther along, he spotted a broken branch. He added that to his arsenal as well. They weren't much, but Mac had practiced fighting with less.

Not long after that, he found the trail they'd followed the night before. He knew they hadn't walked far on it, so he intended to follow the path downhill only a short way before returning to the unmarked woods. The smoother passage of the trail let him pick up speed, which he appreciated.

As he walked, Mac kept shifting his focus, trying to see in all directions at once. He hadn't forgotten the bear from the night before. He had read that bears were most active in morning and evening, so the possibility of running into it on the trail was considerably stronger than he cared to dwell on, especially since the animal tracked them the night before.

With the bear constantly in his thoughts, Mac startled when he came upon a shape on the trail, and it took a moment for reality to set in.

It wasn't a bear sprawled on the trail. It was the gunman who'd shot at the animal last night.

And the man was dead.

11

When he'd seen the bear near the cave, Mac assumed that the gunman's shot had wounded the animal and driven it away. He'd been wrong. He knelt beside the body to examine it. Though the man's clothes were torn and his face scratched, a bulletproof vest had offered him considerable protection against the bear's attack. But Mac could see that the gunman had died from a broken neck, probably the result of a single blow from the bear's paw.

He rose slowly to his feet. Unless the two gunmen they'd encountered at Ginny's house had called in reinforcements, there was only a single armed man in the woods. That would improve his odds. He also had to consider the possibility that the second gunman had fled when he found his partner dead.

I know almost nothing for certain, he reminded himself. He had to stay on his guard.

Mac left the body and continued moving as quietly as possible down the trail. With a few hours of sleep behind him and an insuppressible hope that they could make it out of the forest alive, Mac found the trail an easy and surprisingly beautiful walk. He heard birds singing in the trees all around him.

Though he tried to keep his mind attuned to danger, it insisted upon dragging him to thoughts of Ginny. He would never say anything to her, but he knew he had developed feelings for her. *It's perfectly normal,* he told himself. When men and women worked together in life-threatening situations, it often created heightened emotions.

He couldn't trust those emotions, so he pressed them down as ruthlessly as he could manage. He and Ginny were radically different people, and he was not going to forget that in some stress-induced romantic haze.

Eventually Mac reluctantly left the trail. He had no idea where the path led when followed downhill, but since Ginny had moved cross-country to reach it the night before, he assumed it wouldn't take him where he wanted to go. He slipped between the trees and let gravity lead him down, hoping he'd left the trail at the right location.

The combination of his downhill trajectory and the bright morning sun offered considerably more of a view than he'd had the night before, when he'd climbed the hill behind Ginny. That increased field of vision kept him from missing the lawyer's cabin entirely. He caught a glimmer of light on glass and detoured toward it.

When he saw the cabin through the trees, he felt a jolt of excitement, but he didn't allow it to push him into foolishness. Instead, he took a zigzag path, moving from tree to tree and pausing behind each one to watch and listen. Though he couldn't claim his passage was silent, it was as close as he could manage, and he'd come to understand that the woods offered plenty of background noise. All around him birds sang, squirrels bickered, and brush rustled.

When Mac could see most of the cabin, he stopped to study the area. The door to the cabin was open, which Mac found ominous. He was certain he had closed it behind them. It wasn't shocking to think that the gunmen had found the cabin and broken in. In their position, he would have done the same thing. But why leave the door open? The yawning darkness beyond the doorframe reminded Mac of the open mouth of something hungry. That darkness would be the perfect place to lie in wait.

But why lurk in such an obvious spot? If the gunmen had entered the cabin—and they must have—they would have seen evidence that the people they were after had come and gone. He thought of the drawings Benji had made. They were probably still on the table, which meant anyone searching the house would have proof the child had been there. The same drawings were at Ginny's cabin, unless she'd carried them away with her.

If the gunmen knew that their quarry had come and gone, would they expect them to return? Mac had no answer to that. The unanswered questions in his brain were beginning to stack up to annoying heights. Why was the door open? How many gunmen were hunting them? Who had sent them and why? Questions without answers did no good, so Mac swatted them away like mosquitoes and began to creep toward the house, keeping low and moving slow. With any luck, he wasn't stepping into his last minutes, and he would be able to fulfill his promise to his nephew.

Having never been good at standing around and doing nothing, Ginny immediately began to tidy the cave. She'd pack up everything they didn't immediately need and make a plan for the day. She remembered a creek nearby and longed for the chance to wash her face and hands, even if the water was as icy as she remembered. But she couldn't risk leaving the cave. She pulled the band from her hair and ran a hand through it. It felt powdery from the dust and dirt she'd picked up. As she finger-combed away the snarls, she considered fishing for the mirror she kept in her duffel. On the other hand, seeing her present state would likely do nothing to brighten her mood.

Though the crack that gave them access to the cave didn't offer much sunlight, it also meant light from the cave wouldn't be obvious from outside. So she pulled a small battery-powered lantern from her bag. The lantern telescoped in on itself to make packing easier. She tugged it open, then switched it on. Though it didn't banish all of the shadows in the cave, it did make the interior far less gloomy and lacked the creepiness of the green chemical light she'd used the night before.

Benji abandoned the snakeskin he'd discovered and walked over to squat next to the lamp, examining it with interest.

"It's nice to have some light," Ginny said.

Benji didn't respond.

"You've been awfully brave through all this."

He shook his head.

She smiled. "You think you're not brave because you feel scared." His head bobbed, but he kept his attention fixed on the lantern. "I'm scared too, and so is Mac. Bravery has nothing to do with being scared. When scary things happen, normal people get scared."

That finally drew his eyes to her, his expression doubtful.

She laughed. "Honestly, you can trust me. I know all about normal."

The corner of one side of his mouth twitched upward. It wasn't exactly a grin, but it was a sign of interest, and she'd take it. "Bravery is really about what you *do* when you're scared. You've done a lot of brave things on this trip. You haven't quit. And that's brave. Doing what you need to do, no matter how you feel, is brave."

Benji made no response to that, and Ginny wasn't sure if he believed what she'd told him, but she figured he'd think about it. She couldn't hope for much more. Still, it wouldn't do for him to spend the hours ahead brooding. She couldn't take him outside for a wander, but she could come up with a distraction.

"Want to play a game?"

His eyes met hers again, bright with curiosity.

"I know of a game that's been played for a long, long time. We'll need some pebbles. About this big." She held her thumb and forefinger about half an inch apart. "A handful, if you can find them."

He darted around and soon retrieved a small stone. He held it out to show her. "Right, that's a perfect size. As many of those as you can find."

He scurried around, collecting small stones. She knew giving him something to do was the best medicine to combat fear.

While Benji gathered pebbles, she sorted through the contents of her duffel, surveying what they would need if they stayed in the cave for another day. She didn't have much food left. She'd never factored in the need to feed the bears in the area. If Mac was gone for more than a few hours, she would have to go out and search for something to eat. Mentally, she began listing edible things she could find nearby, wondering if she would be able to talk Benji into eating bugs.

She was distracted by a tap on her arm. Benji held out a small handful of pebbles. "Those are perfect," she said, letting him pour the pebbles into her hand. She slipped them into her jacket pocket, the same pocket that had held the pepper. "I think we need about that many more, and we'll be able to play."

She expected Benji to return to hunting pebbles, but instead he pivoted and pointed toward the far corner of the cave, not far from where he and Mac had slept. "Did you see something?" she asked. He tugged on her sleeve, then walked over to the wall and pointed again.

Ginny stood, ignoring the popping of her knees and the aches in her back and neck. She crossed the cave, recognizing before she reached him what Benji meant. She was amazed that she could have forgotten about something that had been so important to her when she was Benji's age.

In the far wall, another crack led out of the cavern. It was far too small for Ginny to pass through now. Even Benji would have to wriggle, but she remembered the feel of the rocks pressing on her as she squirmed through long ago, bent on new adventure and discovery.

"There is another cavern through there," she told him. "It's not as big as this one, but I used to play in it when I was your age. There's a vein of quartz in the wall in there. It's really pretty when a flashlight shines on it."

Benji's eyes lit up, and he scooted closer to the crack. She felt an immediate thrill of worry, remembering the snakeskin that still lay on the cave floor several feet away. Whatever snake had left the skin could potentially be in the cavern beyond. Then she discarded the idea. Snakes probably did pass winter in the cavern, where the temperature stayed fairly steady, but during the warmer months, the snakes would find the cave cold compared to the outside world, and not nearly as rich in food.

Impulsively she pulled the flashlight from her other jacket pocket and held it out to Benji. "You can go check it out. But be careful. I haven't been in there since I outgrew the entrance."

He nodded eagerly and took the flashlight. He squatted and aimed the flashlight through the crack, peering after it. He reminded Ginny so sharply of herself that she felt curious along with him—a need to see what lay out of sight. Despite what they'd been through over the last twenty-four hours, despite what Benji had been through with the death of his parents, he still had the burning wonder of any other little boy. That was a very good sign.

He crawled into the crack, and Ginny had to fight the urge to pull him toward her to keep him safe. Whatever was in the next cavern, he would benefit from the opportunity to face it and come out triumphant. It would be more therapeutic than anything else she could offer him now. So she made a point of moving away to pack the emergency blankets for her duffel. Even if they ended up in the cavern for another night, it was better to be ready to leave in an instant.

She folded the blankets, matching the original folds exactly. It wasn't necessary, but something about the precision and order comforted her. She didn't have many sources of comfort. Mac was off in the woods, and she had no way of knowing whether she would see him again. Benji was out of sight, and though her brain knew he was probably completely safe, it didn't do much to calm her fears.

"I've gotten attached," she murmured under her breath. It wasn't wise for a therapist to get attached to patients, though it was hard to avoid when the people in need were children. With a sigh, she crammed the blankets into her duffel, then headed across the room to grab Alan's sweater, a little worse for wear since the ordeal she'd put it through last night.

Her head snapped up at the sound of a crack outside. Someone or something was out there. It could be Mac, returning for who knew what reason. It could also be the bear, lumbering around in search of more cereal bars.

But it could also be something a lot worse.

Ginny shifted to stand firmly between the crack in the wall that led to the second cavern, where Benji was, and the crack that led outside where someone or something was moving. She considered making a run for the duffel and the shotgun that leaned against the side of the cave, but the sounds had moved through the crack to the cave. Whatever had been outside was coming in, and she didn't have time to arm herself against it.

How could I have been so careless?

Her heart thudded in her chest, and she wished so hard to hear Mac's voice, but she knew better. Mac would have spoken up already to assuage her fear.

She spun to press her face against the crack through which Benji had gone. "Stay hidden," she whispered. She got no response, but she had to trust that Benji heard her. Nothing else was acceptable.

Ginny was on her feet, back against the wall, when a man stepped through into the cavern. He was smaller than Mac, so had probably found the passage considerably easier, though his face still bore the signs of a scrape against the rocks, and his dark jeans and sweater were dusted with gray. The expression he wore was as cold and harsh as the barrel of the gun pointed at her chest.

"Hold it right there," he said.

And faced with no other choice, she obeyed.

12

The urge to glance back and ensure Benji was still hidden nearly overwhelmed her, but Ginny resisted. The smallest indication of Benji's location could draw the gunman's attention. Whatever happened to her, she had to keep the child safe.

Ginny raised her chin defiantly. "Who are you? What do you want?"

The man ignored her questions, though she saw his eyes dart around, checking out the contents of the cave. She was extremely glad she'd cleaned up. There was nothing in the cave to tell him anything. "Where's Macklin and the kid?"

Ginny huffed. "Gone," she said as coldly as she could manage. "We split up. I wasn't going to be slowed down by a crying kid." *I don't mean it, Benji.*

Again the man's eyes darted around, but he couldn't refute Ginny's words, and she knew it. The cave offered no place to hide a man as big as Mac, and the small cracks in the walls appeared too tight for anyone, even a child as small as Benji, to pass through. But the man's attention sharpened on her again, his eyes narrow. "Gone where?"

She lifted a shoulder in a shrug, as if to convey how little she cared. "Last I knew, they were heading to the ranger station. I didn't want to be in the woods in the dark, so I figured I'd wait in here. You two had to leave sometime."

The man shook his head. "That's a lie."

"Really?" she said, pretending to misunderstand as she shoved her hands nonchalantly into her pockets. "Are you planning to buy a cabin here?"

The man growled, and Ginny was suddenly reminded that he had a gun. Something in his expression suggested he would enjoy shooting her. Fear lanced through her, but she knew better than to let it show. He'd try to manipulate that fear if he became aware of it, so she could not let him know how much that gun made her want to roll into a ball and whimper.

"I've been to the ranger station," the man said. "They were the ones who told me about this cave. Not that they did so willingly, of course." The man took several steps closer, clearly intending to appear menacing but actually giving her some hope. There was nothing she could do to fight him off when he was so far away. "You're going to tell me where Macklin and the kid went, or I'm going to hurt you until you do."

"Don't hurt me," she whispered, leading the man to step closer still. Her fingers wrapped around the pebbles in her pocket.

The man opened his mouth to issue another threat, and Ginny yanked her hand from her pocket, hurling the handful of pebbles into the man's face before diving for the floor. He yelped and grabbed for his eyes with his free hand, but Ginny wasn't finished. She didn't have a weapon. But she had never skipped leg day at the gym, and she kicked him, putting all the strength she had into the motion. Her foot connected with the side of his knee, and the sound it made was sickening.

The man went down, screaming. When he hit the ground, the gun went off with a roar that was deafening in the enclosed space. The muzzle was pointed nowhere near Ginny, so she was in no danger from the shot itself, but she ducked—worried the bullet might ricochet against the cave walls—and the shock of the noise made her head spin. She moved again, not wanting the man to guess where she was and better aim the gun. Besides, she needed a weapon of her own.

The shotgun was still too far away, but the lantern was close at hand. She grabbed the handle and rose up again, swinging the lantern into the side of the man's head. He never saw it coming, as he was on his knees, clawing at his face and waving the handgun around wildly. The lantern wasn't as heavy as she'd prefer, but it had sharp edges, and they opened up a sizable cut on the side of the man's forehead, making him cry out anew.

Ginny spotted movement across the cavern. Benji had slipped out of the crack in the wall and was running for the gap that led outside. The man on the floor hadn't seen him. She doubted he could see much at all between the pebbles and the blood from his head wound.

Despite the advantage of partially blinding the gunman, Ginny wasn't going to risk him discovering Benji before the child had escaped, so she snagged the strap of her duffel. She scrambled to her feet and pivoted. The man was struggling to get up on his one good leg, but Ginny swung the heavy duffel, holding the strap with both hands. The momentum was impressive, and she felt the bag connect with a shock that ran through both her arms.

The man went down. Benji had gotten away, and Ginny decided it was time for her to do so as well. She couldn't leave the child alone in the woods with another gunman out there. She didn't even go after the shotgun, since it wasn't in the path of her sprint toward the cave opening. She couldn't afford the detour. She didn't have much time before the gunman followed.

She ran for the crack, the duffel still in her hand, and shoved herself through without hesitation.

"Stop!" the man shouted behind her. He fired again, and the roar was less painful as she was already through the crack, but the bullet hit close enough that she felt a stinging spray of broken rock against the back of her head.

She ignored it and kept moving. Benji needed her.

Though the trip to the front door was one of the longest Mac had ever made, he finally convinced himself that the lack of movement from inside the cabin meant it was safe to enter. He slipped in and found the cabin mostly as they'd left it. A small table had been knocked over, and the pottery vase that had stood on it lay smashed on the floor. As Mac studied the mess, he realized one of their pursuers must have taken out his frustration on the piece of furniture.

"Good," Mac muttered under his breath. Frustration could make them reckless. He ignored the fact that it could also make them more dangerous.

Mac quickly checked the bedroom and bathroom, mostly in the interest of being thorough. He snagged a bottle of water from a case sitting on one of the kitchen counters and downed it quickly. They hadn't been able to carry all the water away with them, and he knew it was wise to take the opportunity to hydrate while he could.

With the door to the cabin hanging open, the interior of the main room was considerably brighter than it had been when Mac, Ginny, and Benji had hidden inside. But the increased light didn't reveal any happy surprises—such as an undiscovered satellite phone—so he left the building behind and trotted across the yard toward the shed.

He reached the door of the other structure, happy for the partial concealment offered by an overgrown shrub.

Mac glared at the latch and lock on the door. They were untouched. The men tracking them must not have bothered with the shed, much to Mac's disappointment. He could have used the help getting in. But then the men might have taken or disabled the ATV inside, and then where would he be?

He pulled on the hanging lock and saw that the door and latch were high quality. There was no way he could simply use brute force to knock it off without a tool.

He glanced toward the cabin, wondering if there was something inside he could use to pry off the latch. It was possible, but he wasn't sure he could waste the time searching. Besides, if Ginny had seen a pry bar in the cabin, she'd have mentioned it or taken it with her.

Maybe he'd be lucky and the lawyer had left the key to the lock nearby.

First, Mac checked in all the usual spots. He reached along the upper edge of the door frame and found nothing but dirt and a handful of spiderwebs. More unnerved than he'd care to admit, he quickly wiped the clinging matter onto the leaves of his concealing shrub.

Mac scanned the ground around the shed, searching for a rock that could serve as a hiding place for the key. He never thought the fake key rocks were all that convincing, but he stopped to flip over a few suspiciously round stones anyway. They were all real and hid nothing more exciting than crickets. Mac peered at the cabin. Maybe the lawyer kept the key in a drawer.

But do I have time to search for it?

He'd hated leaving Ginny and Benji. Their absence felt like the countdown of a time bomb, with each passing second increasing his tension. Mac shook himself. He wasn't usually given to indecision. Squaring his shoulders, he ran for the cabin again. He'd check a couple of drawers, fast.

The kitchen offered a drawer full of the kinds of odds and ends that tend to accrue in such places—stray screws, batteries in a variety of sizes, bits of wire, scraps of paper, and two unidentified keys. With a grin of triumph, Mac snatched them up and headed back toward the shed. He tried both in the padlock and nearly shouted with frustration when neither fit. He almost threw them away, spurred on by the same frustration, then realized one of them might start the ATV inside the shed. He could hot-wire the vehicle, but having the key would be nice.

But he still had to get inside. He thought of the tools stashed in his SUV, but there was no time for that. He needed to get inside the shed immediately. Considering the rocks he'd flipped over earlier, Mac grabbed the largest. He hefted the stone in his hand, shifting it for the best grip as well as a nice sharp edge.

His right arm was thickly wrapped in a bandage, but he doubted that would offer enough protection against flying glass, so he switched the rock to his left hand and pulled his leather jacket sleeve down to cover as much as possible. Then he turned his back to the window and raised his bandaged arm to shield his face. He swung his left arm and the rock struck the window glass, smashing through it spectacularly.

He shifted the rock back to his right hand and used the edge to knock out any remaining shards of glass clinging to the frame. The window wasn't large, and he'd need all the space cleared in order to wriggle through. One thing he didn't need was to slice open a vein as he climbed in.

With the window clear, Mac once again considered entering the cabin. If he grabbed a chair, he could use it to boost himself through the hole at a better angle. He was likely to fall the last few feet onto a glass-covered floor, so maybe he should find something to wrap around his hands to protect them against the landing. He imagined a fancy lawyer probably had a drawer full of cashmere scarves that would do the trick.

"I'm almost there," he said, trying to calm the panic that nagged at him constantly. He'd crawl through the window and then knock down the door from the inside where the sound would be slightly muffled. If all else failed, he'd try to knock down the door with the help of the ATV.

"First things first," he said. "Chair and scarves." He'd barely stepped around the wild shrub when he heard a gunshot. Instinct nearly sent him to the ground to avoid being an easy target, but his brain overrode that idea. The shot hadn't come from nearby. It came from farther up the mountain.

In fact, he was positive it came from the direction of Ginny's cave.

"No," Mac said, not bothering to whisper. "No, no, no." And without another second of hesitation or a glance toward the shed, he sprinted toward the woods.

13

All of Mac's training—keeping low, not offering an obvious target, and moving slowly—was tossed away as he ran across the open yard of the cabin and burst into the woods. With the steady climb upward, he kept as fast a pace as he could. A part of him knew he risked tripping, falling, even breaking an ankle, but he didn't care.

Sometimes he felt as if he lost as much ground as he gained when he hit soft soil and slid downhill for several feet before grabbing a branch or sapling and heading up again. More than once he pushed on a branch only to have it slap him hard across the face. Each time, he knew his reckless speed could cost him, but there was no choice. Someone had fired a gun, and he had to see that Ginny and Benji were okay.

Finally, he spotted a white blaze on the side of a pine tree and knew he was on the trail. At last he could really move, but he hadn't gone far before he heard the sound of someone running toward him.

Ginny and Benji burst into view, making a turn on the path sharply enough that Ginny had to help Benji keep his footing. Tears stung Mac's eyes as soon as he realized they were both unharmed.

But Ginny didn't stop to chat. She plowed right past him and continued down the trail with Benji's hand in hers, gasping out a few words. "Gunman. At cave. Following."

"Keep going," Mac said, though he knew the advice was unnecessary. He didn't follow them but instead moved quickly along the way they'd come. He was done running away. He'd tried that and had nearly gotten Ginny and Benji killed. It was time to take the offensive and put a stop to whatever was going on.

Mac grabbed another stout branch—unsure where he'd lost his last one—and moved on, not running but not hesitating either. As he walked, he took deep, slow breaths, bringing his body under control. He'd need to be smart and fast if he hoped to survive the coming encounter.

He stepped off the path and continued moving parallel to it, so he wouldn't be directly in the route of whoever was following Ginny and Benji. He darted from tree to tree, giving himself as much cover as he could find. He had paused behind a sturdy oak and stood on a rock for a better viewpoint when he spotted movement further up the trail. A man came into view. His face was filthy and bloody and he limped heavily, almost hobbling. Mac smiled tightly and whispered, "Good for you, Ginny."

While he worked out the best spot to ambush the man, he spotted something else—something so surprising he almost laughed out loud. In a beam of warm morning light, a snake sunbathed, its length stretched out across the path. The creature's mottled diamond pattern had made it hard to spot at first, but it also made it easy to identify. A rattlesnake.

Very slowly, Mac slipped through the trees, keeping cover between himself and the man on the trail. He found a wide tree close to the path, not far from the sunning snake, then squatted down to make the most of the concealing brush and waited, hoping the snake continued its sunbathing for a bit longer.

Mac's breath was shallow, and his body almost quivered with tension as he waited. Cramps threatened in his calves, but he shifted very little to relieve the pressure. He couldn't risk being seen.

After what felt like a long few minutes, he heard the man moving down the path. He shifted his gaze to the snake, concerned it might slither away. After all, he'd read that snakes were sensitive to vibration, but if the snake cared about the coming man, it showed no sign.

The meeting of man and snake was as spectacular as Mac could have hoped. The man shrieked at the sight of the snake and sprang backward, landing on his bad leg, which folded under him. He crumpled to the ground with another cry of pain.

The rattler responded to the movement by coiling up quickly and trying to warn the man off with ominous rattling. The man was in no condition to flee though, and merely scooted awkwardly away, aiming his handgun at the snake.

Mac slipped through the trees as the man's attention remained on the snake. He winced as the man began firing at the rattler in a panic, but he didn't stop. He popped out on the trail behind the man and bashed him across the shoulders and neck with a branch he'd grabbed. The man dropped the gun, then scrabbled to find it again. Not giving him time to recover, Mac tackled him, knocking him away from the gun.

As they wrestled, the man kept shrieking that there was a snake, making it plain he was much more afraid of the rattlesnake than he was of Mac. As a result, Mac recovered the gun rather easily and pointed it at the terrified man.

His captive stared around the trail. "Where's the snake?"

"I expect we scared it off," Mac said. "Why didn't you shoot it?"

"I tried," the man yelled. "We have to get out of here."

"I don't think so." Mac searched the man and was delighted to find flex cuffs, which he used to bind the man's hands and feet.

"Come on. I can't walk all trussed up like this," the man complained.

"Not a problem," Mac said. "You're not going anywhere."

"You can't leave me here," the man protested. "There's a snake."

Mac felt certain the snake was far away, but he asked, "Did it bite you?"

"No," the man said. "I don't think so."

"It can be hard to tell," Mac told him. "Snake venom has an ingredient that kills the pain. That way you walk around and get the blood pumping. The venom hits your heart and..." He shrugged. *"Bam."* Mac knew the lie was outrageous, but the man was so panicked and so inexperienced with snakes that he bought it completely.

"You have to check me over," the man begged. "See if I'm bitten. Or better yet, get me to the hospital."

"Get you to the hospital?" Mac echoed. "You do remember that you and your buddy shot up my SUV."

"You have to save me. I can feel the poison in my heart."

That would be panic. Mac shrugged. "I will consider helping you. I may carry you down the mountain if you answer some questions for me."

"Anything."

"Who hired you to come after us?"

The man's face paled. "I don't know. Honest. I was recruited by a business I'd applied to months ago. I didn't get the job because I had a record."

"But then they called you? What business is this?"

The man swallowed hard. "Macklin Security."

Mac groaned, then started to walk away. "If you're going to lie, you can stay here."

"I'm not lying! It was Macklin Security in New York City."

"Yeah, I know where the company is. Who specifically hired you?"

"I don't know. I got a phone call and the guy on the other end didn't identify himself, except to say he was from Macklin Security. He said they'd reconsidered my application and I could have the job if I proved myself."

"Proved yourself by coming after us?"

"Yeah." The man was so eager to tell the story he stumbled over his words. "It was me and another new hire. We were sent here to take out a security threat—terrorists."

"Just the two of you?"

The man's head bobbed eagerly.

Mac stared coldly into his desperate, sweaty face and felt a building fury. "You believed a six-year-old child was a terrorist."

The man swallowed hard. "Sometimes terrorists use kids as cover. I've seen it on TV, and the man from Macklin Security said that was happening here." The man stopped talking, his eyes widening at the expression on Mac's face. "Hey, I wasn't going to hurt the kid. We would have taken him safely to Macklin Security."

Mac narrowed his eyes. If the two men had truly cared about Benji's safety for even a second, they wouldn't have shot into a building with Benji inside. They had no way of knowing whether they'd hit the child or not.

"Fine," Mac said. He spun on his heel and started down the path.

"Hey, wait!" the bound man shouted. "You can't abandon me here. You said you'd carry me down the mountain."

Mac didn't look back. "I lied."

Once they'd passed Mac, Ginny slowed her pace slightly, aware that she was in danger of simply dragging Benji along the ground if she kept running. A six-year-old couldn't hope to keep up that pace. She hated that Mac hadn't fallen in behind them, but she knew their survival could depend on whether he could handle the shooter behind them.

Security is Mac's job, she reminded herself as they walked. That line went through her mind over and over, as if believing it hard enough could somehow keep Mac safe. She almost found herself lulled into believing it when gunshots rang out from above. She grabbed Benji and carried him off the trail, away from the line of fire.

The pattern of the gunshots sounded almost wild. Ginny hoped that was a good sign, but she couldn't completely get rid of the image of Mac wounded and bleeding. She couldn't go back. She had to do what was best for Benji.

She kept an arm around him as they slid down the side of the mountain, no longer sticking to the gentler slope of the trail. Benji tugged on her sleeve and pointed upward toward the sound of the shots. He knew what they meant as well as she did.

"I know, buddy," she murmured. "We have to stay away from there."

Their rapid descent was dangerous, but she didn't dare slow down. If Mac didn't stop the gunman, their only hope was to put enough distance between them. She tried to think as they wove between trees. She could try to complete Mac's plan. She knew how to drive an ATV, and if Mac had slowed the man enough, she and the boy could reach safety.

Her other alternative would be to go to her cabin. That assumed the second gunman hadn't stayed there in case they returned. She hadn't seen him. She had no way of knowing where he was. *This is a situation where what you don't know can definitely hurt you—or worse.*

She decided on the ATV. It was closer, and there was always the possibility Mac had gotten it out of the shed before he heard the gunshots. He'd had considerable time. If the ATV was already easily available, that would be their best chance.

A stitch in Ginny's side left her gasping, and she ducked behind a thick oak.

Benji immediately tried to climb up the hill, but she caught him by the arm. "We can't," she said. "We have to get off the mountain and get help."

The boy frowned fiercely at her and pointed up the hill.

"I know. I'm worried about Mac too, but he's tougher than we are."

Benji shook his head and pointed at her.

She laughed softly in response. "No, I think Mac is probably tougher than me too. We'll go get the police. It's what he would want us to do. It's what he would want you to do. He wouldn't want you to put yourself in danger."

Benji pressed his lips together, but he stopped fighting her. Instead, he just sat on the ground. She left him alone to sort out his feelings while she pressed a hand hard against the cramp in her side and slowed her breathing as well as she could.

Finally, she held out a hand. "We need to go to my friend's cabin. That's where Mac was going. We can take the ATV and leave."

Benji frowned, and Ginny guessed why. "An ATV is like a motorcycle, but it's wider and has four wheels. You'll enjoy it."

He perked up, interested, and she levered herself away from the tree. He took her hand, and they continued heading down. Despite their wild run, they hadn't gotten far off track, and she was able to adjust quickly. When they finally reached the clearing where Alan's cabin stood, Ginny immediately spotted the open cabin door. Had Mac done that?

She flinched at the sight of the yawning darkness. She crouched down so she could speak quietly to the boy. "Benji, I need to check the area. Can you stay here?"

He frowned but shrugged in what she assumed was agreement. "Promise?"

He nodded. She hated to leave him for even a short time, but if she moved into the clearing, she'd be an easy target if the second gunman was still in the house. She pointed to a thick patch of brush. "You can hide in there. Then no one will see you until I call you."

He obviously wasn't happy, but he headed for the brush. She skirted the edge of the clearing, staying in the shadows as much as possible until she reached the shed. She found a broken window, but no sign that Mac had gotten inside. She still didn't know if the ATV was in working order, and she had no idea how to get it out of the shed. The door was secure, and the padlock bore no sign of rust. How had Mac intended to get the ATV out of there?

She'd never get the vehicle out of the shed without making enough noise to bring the bad guys straight to her. It wasn't a solution after all. Moving silently from tree to tree and keeping out of sight of the cabin as much as possible, she returned to Benji's hiding place.

The relief on the boy's face was evident when he crawled out of the brush to join her. "We can't get the ATV," she whispered to him. "We're going to my cabin."

She didn't know whether it was safer, but she was beginning to doubt that "safe" was an option available to them, no matter what they did. But if her cabin was unguarded, she could make it to her small garage and get her car. Odds were, the shooters hadn't gotten into the garage. It was even more secure than the cabin.

I guess you can take the girl out of the paranoid family, but you can't take the paranoia out of the girl.

Benji seemed content to get moving, and he followed her through the woods without resistance. He appeared to have given up on the idea of going back to find his uncle. The thought of that made her heart hurt. Benji was too young to have to be that pragmatic.

They had nearly reached the cabin when Ginny heard a sound behind them. She pulled Benji against a tree trunk and peered through the trees and brush. She couldn't see anything moving, but she'd definitely heard something.

It could be a deer, she supposed. It was late morning, probably a little too late for most deer to be out wandering, but it wasn't impossible. With so few humans around, deer had far less to fear in the woods.

It could also be the bear they'd encountered. That would be far more dangerous, but also more likely. A bear would be drawn to the cabins and the possibility of food.

Of course, the answer could be a lot more obvious. Ginny carefully slipped a hand into her duffel and felt around until she found the knife secure in its sheath. She flipped the snap on the sheath with one finger and slipped the knife out of the bag. Whether a bear or a man followed them, Ginny was willing to do whatever she must to defend them.

Benji clung to her sleeve, and she touched his head gently, then held up a hand, signaling him to stay. She would take the fight to whatever was following them.

She wasn't confused about the value of a knife, even one as sharp as hers, in a gunfight. She was quick, and she had both training and experience, but she wasn't bulletproof. Her sole advantage would come if she could go after the man before he knew she was there. She knew she was better at moving quietly in the forest.

And she wouldn't hesitate to strike first for the sake of the little boy with large eyes who waited in silence behind her.

14

As he raced down the mountainside, Mac was nearly crazed with worry, knowing Ginny must have heard the gunshots and imagined the worst. His first thought was that she might have gone up the mountain to the ranger station, but he discarded that quickly. It would be slow, especially with a child, and she wouldn't risk it. That left down the mountain, or toward the ATV.

If the man he'd left bound had spoken the truth, they didn't have to worry about any more gunmen, unless whoever had set the whole situation in motion had sent in additional killers after not hearing from the first two. He pushed aside everything else the man had said. Mac had no proof that whoever sent them was connected to Macklin Security. Anyone could say they were from his company. It was equally true that the gunman could simply have lied. He'd been desperate, but that didn't mean he was honest. Either way, Mac would think about it later. For the time being, he had to find Ginny and Benji.

If Ginny thought Mac had been shot and the killer was after her and Benji again, she'd be moving the two of them as quickly as she could rather than taking the time to keep cover in the thick trees, so hopefully they'd be easier to spot. Benji would limit their speed, but they had a solid head start on Mac, and he was merely guessing that they'd head for the ATV.

As he moved through rough terrain, climbing over deadfall and avoiding thorns in the undergrowth, Mac's body protested. He was exhausted, and everything hurt. The bear's scratches on his arm were especially painful, and he shoved aside worry that the wounds were infected. Infected or not, he couldn't let them slow him down.

Suddenly Mac skidded to a halt as he realized he should have hit the clearing for the lawyer's cabin by now. He must have gotten off course somehow in his haste to catch up. He stood frozen, listening intently, even though he knew the chances of Ginny making enough noise for him to hear were slim. Still, if she cranked up the ATV, he would certainly hear that. *Sure, and you may even get there in time to see them ride off without you.*

Annoyed that he'd let himself get lost, Mac did what he knew was the worst possible thing when lost in the woods—he picked a direction and headed that way, hoping he'd chosen correctly. As he trudged along, he imagined Ginny making it to civilization and needing to send a rescue party to find him in the woods. The thought wasn't as upsetting as he'd expected, since it began with Ginny and Benji making it to safety. If he had to wander around for a while longer, it wouldn't be the end of the world.

To his surprise and relief, he soon spotted the cabin. He'd chosen correctly after all. The door to the cabin still hung open, and he doubted Ginny would take Benji inside and leave it like that. He watched the dark opening for a moment but saw no movement, so he slipped around the clearing toward the shed. He knew he could have just walked across the clearing, but he couldn't quite give up the impulse to move carefully, again reminding himself that the man he'd captured could have been lying or wrong about how many people were after the trio.

The shed was still locked up with the ATV inside. He passed the building, pondering where to go next. Had he guessed wrong entirely? Could Ginny have gone up to the ranger station? That felt wrong. Heading for her cabin, especially considering there might be more surprises there than she's shared with him so far, seemed more logical.

He went straight across the clearing and plunged into the woods on the other side of the cabin.

He hadn't gone far before he spotted something that nearly made him shout with relief—a small shoe print pressed into a patch of soft mud. He was on the right track. He was positively grinning as he picked up speed. He wasn't sure what Ginny and Benji would do next. One thing was certain—his SUV was in no condition to drive. He could have changed one tire, but the gunmen had probably shot out all four, and there was no way they'd get off the mountain running on the rims. Ginny must have a car there somewhere. He guessed that was what she was after.

His grin widened as he thought that they could be on the verge of getting out of the whole mess. He pushed through a stand of brush—and gave a shout of surprise as Ginny exploded from around a thick tree and rushed at him, wielding a knife.

He ducked, grateful that exhaustion and injury hadn't completely dulled the reflexes he'd honed from years in the security business. "Ginny, it's me!"

She stumbled to a stop, her momentum nearly sending her plunging into him despite herself. Mac had to catch her arm to keep her from falling. Her eyes, wide with shock, were nearly as big as Benji's. "Ginny," he said again.

She took a shuddering breath, then burst into tears. Mac gathered her to his chest and held her as she sobbed. She fit against him as if they'd embraced many times before, and something about holding her felt natural and right. Benji joined them, and Mac was touched to see his nephew patting Ginny's back as she cried, the child's own eyes dry.

"The gunmen have both been taken care of," Mac told her gently. "The bear got one of them, and I tied up the other. We're going to be okay. It's okay now."

As Mac explained that the gunshots they'd heard were aimed at a snake, not at him, she tried to nod, but her forehead bumped his chest. She knew she should move away from Mac, but she couldn't stop crying. It was as if all the tension of the past twenty-four hours had melted into a river determined to run down her face. She didn't want to be seen while she was so out of control.

When her mental equilibrium finally reset, she pushed away from him, rubbing her eyes with the heels of her hands. "Sorry," she said, her voice husky. She looked down at Benji. "Sorry about that."

Benji smiled, his expression sunnier than she'd ever seen it before.

"You don't need to be sorry," Mac said firmly. "You've been amazing. You kept Benji safe, and I suspect you're the reason we're all still alive. The gunman I tied up said there were only the two of them, so we should be able to get off the mountain without being shot at anymore."

"We can take my car," Ginny said.

"If those guys didn't sabotage it too," Mac said. "The SUV is in bad shape."

"I doubt they could have gotten to it. It's this way." She tried for her usual confident tone, but she knew her voice was still affected by her crying spell.

"Well, now you know about the gunshots you heard," Mac said. "You want to tell me about the one I heard?"

"Oh, from the cave. Right." Ginny was stunned at how long ago that felt when, in reality, it had probably been less than an hour. "It seems that gunman you tied up had been to the ranger station. They told him about the cave, and he came to check it out. Thankfully, Benji had crawled through to a smaller second cavern so he was safe." She glanced at the boy who walked between Mac and her. "And he was smart enough to stay put until exactly the right time."

Benji beamed at the praise.

"So who was the guy shooting at?" Mac asked.

"Technically me," Ginny said. "But he didn't come all that close." She didn't bother to say she probably still had rocks and dirt in her hair from exactly how close the bullet had come.

"I should have kicked him a few times after I tied him up," Mac grumbled.

"No, you shouldn't," Ginny said. "More than that, I know you wouldn't. You're not that kind of person."

"We've known each other barely more than a day, and you know what kind of person I am?" Mac asked.

"I think our time together has been revealing," Ginny said. "Plus, Benji loves you, and he's a great judge of character."

Again, the boy grinned at the compliment.

Without any kind of spoken agreement, they all grew quiet as they approached Ginny's cabin. Ginny wasn't interested in trusting the words of a man who had been willing to shoot her, so they scouted the area around the house carefully to be sure no one was there waiting for them. When the whole area stayed quiet, with no sound but the comforting one of undisturbed birdsong, Ginny pulled her car keys from her duffel where she'd tossed them before they'd jumped into the tunnel a lifetime ago.

Could it really have been barely a day?

She flipped through the keys and found the one to the garage. She'd taught herself long ago to identify each key by shape, even in perfect darkness. Thinking about the fact that she could do it reminded her again that she'd probably always carry a certain amount of baggage from her childhood, though the last day had proven that it wasn't entirely useless.

The large garage door had to be unlocked from the inside before it could be raised. There was a fake lock on the outside to fool would-be intruders. She could see where the gunmen had shot at the lock, probably hoping to get in and disable her car. She smiled grimly at the thought. That was probably the shooting they'd heard from Alan's house. The men must have hated not getting inside.

"They shot out the lock," Mac said. "But why close the door after?"

She shook her head. "They didn't get in."

She walked around the garage. At the rear of the building, brush crowded close to the building, making it difficult to see a door carefully designed to resemble part of the wall. That was where Ginny inserted her key and let them into the garage.

"Very cool," Mac said. "And stunningly paranoid."

She didn't comment. He had a good point. She'd paid a lot to make the garage as secure as possible. The door opened in instead of out so that the bushes crowding against it wouldn't be a problem. She'd made the unusual decision so that no one could ever trap her in the garage by blocking the door from the outside, but it had worked out in her favor.

Once inside, Ginny flipped a light switch near the door, surveyed the space, and called out behind her. "We're alone."

She heard Mac grumble as he pushed through the brush, but Benji darted around him to join Ginny, peering around the garage with interest. "You hungry?" she asked him.

Benji's head bobbed.

Ginny crossed the room to open a small fridge. She grabbed a bottle of fruit juice and a cheese stick. "I keep snacks out here because you never know when you might get hungry." *Or be trapped. Or need to make an escape via the garage.*

Benji's face lit up at the sight of the cheese and juice.

"You got more of those?" Mac asked.

"I have plenty. Help yourself."

She unlocked the car, and Benji hopped into the back seat, happily sipping from the bottle of juice. Ginny opened the glove box and pulled out two cords to charge phones. "I don't know if either of these will fit your phone," she said to Mac, joining him where he stood beside the fridge. "My phone is almost dead, so I'm going to let it charge a while until we reach a spot where we can get a signal."

"Good idea," Mac said as he unscrewed the bottle of juice he'd grabbed from the fridge. "I'll drive."

"I don't think so," Ginny said. "I'm not impressed by the condition of your vehicle."

"That was hardly my fault," Mac said, his tone light. "I'm an excellent driver."

"I'm sure you are. You can show me sometime if you want. In your car."

"Well, I would say I can ride shotgun, but we don't have a shotgun any longer."

Ginny winced. "It's up on the mountain. I had to leave the cave in something of a hurry and didn't manage to grab it."

Mac stepped close to her and picked a twig from her hair, still smiling down at her. "And yet you think you should drive."

"I am an excellent driver," she said, and she smiled despite herself as she heard the echo of his earlier statement. "Besides—and this is the bottom line—it's my car. The person who owns the car decides who gets to drive it. Everyone knows that."

Mac laughed. "You do have a point. And I guess I won't mind the chance to rest."

"Good. I'll unlock the main door if you want to haul it open." Then she paused and frowned. "Which reminds me. How is your arm?"

"It hurts, but we should be out of here soon, and I can worry about it then."

She grabbed his hand and brought his bandaged forearm up where she could see it. The bandage was filthy but still mostly intact. Her first aid kit in the duffel was heavily depleted, but she had another in the trunk. She could take the time to clean and put a fresh bandage on his arm, but she suspected he would resist, and she wanted to get out of there as much as he did.

She reached up to press her hand to his cheek, to feel whether his skin was hot to the touch, but he immediately covered her hand with his own, holding it against his face. "You don't have a fever," she said, hoping she didn't sound as breathless as she suddenly felt.

"Good to know," he replied.

She tugged her hand out from under his. "We need to get going."

"Sounds good."

She put a few feet between them, hoping to regain her composure. Surely she wasn't going to get silly over the man with the worst of the danger over. As she bent to pull the lever that unlocked the garage door, she reminded herself that it wasn't the time to relax. They might be out of immediate danger, but they were far from out of the woods, literally or figuratively. Someone had sent two men to kill them. And that hadn't changed simply because the attempt had failed.

It didn't mean the person was done trying.

15

Mac appreciated the luxury of sitting in a well-padded car seat with his injured arm resting. He twisted to see into the back seat. Benji had fallen asleep, leaning into the corner.

With Benji no longer in danger of being frightened by their conversation, Mac risked telling Ginny the things he didn't want Benji to hear. "The gunman I tied up told me where the order to kill us came from."

She stiffened. "Where?"

"Macklin Security."

She sent him a wide-eyed glance before refocusing on the road. "Isn't that your company? What kind of boss are you?"

"I don't know what to think," Mac said. "I can't imagine anyone who is employed by Macklin doing this. The gunmen never found out who was pulling the strings or even got the person's name, so it could have been someone merely pretending to be with Macklin."

"I suppose that's a possibility," Ginny said slowly. "It also implies they were after you, not me."

"The guy claimed they didn't intend to hurt Benji."

Ginny snorted. "I hope you didn't believe that, because nothing in their behavior supports that."

"No," he said. "I didn't believe it."

"Is there any chance the men were telling the truth? That someone at your own business wants you dead?"

"There's always a chance," he said. "Human nature being what it is. But I can't see it." He went on to relate what the man had said about having applied for work at Macklin and getting rejected, then receiving a call later. "I think it was someone pretending to be associated with Macklin."

"How could someone unrelated to your company have known the man was rejected by Macklin?"

Mac shook his head. "I suppose one of the men who works as a bodyguard for us could have been paid to find that information and hand it over. We don't pass that kind of private data around haphazardly, but it's also not one of our most closely guarded secrets."

"Who handles hiring and firing?" Ginny asked. "You?"

Mac shook his head. "My brother used to recruit when he met someone he thought would be a good fit for the company, but the bulk of hiring is handled by our third partner, Cal. He's got that kind of thing down to a science."

"And how does Cal feel about you?"

"He thinks of me as a brother," Mac said, feeling a rush of defensiveness. "Cal was Derrick's best friend since they were kids. We brought him into the company because he's family."

"As a security expert, you must be aware of the frequency with which family members harm one another."

Mac crossed his arms over his chest, then winced when the wounds in his forearm protested. "Forget Cal. I've known him practically all his life, and you couldn't meet a less violent person. He's a skinny kid who wears T-shirts and thick glasses."

Ginny didn't respond to that, but Mac suspected she had more to say and was choosing to be diplomatic, which was surprising in and of itself. He shifted his attention away from her toward the road, then sat up sharply. "Hey, shouldn't we be heading downhill?"

"We're going to the ranger station."

"Did we discuss that?"

"No."

"Shouldn't we?"

"The gunman you've been quoting about his employer also chatted with me in the cave. He said he'd been to the ranger station, and that was how he knew where to look for us. That suggests there may be people up there in need of medical help."

"Or beyond help," Mac said darkly. He twisted to check Benji again, but the boy was still sleeping. "I want to get my nephew off this mountain. We can send help for the rangers."

"I respect your concern for your nephew. I even share it, but I can't ignore the possibility that there could be people in the ranger station who wouldn't survive the delay. On top of that, they may have the ability to call for help from there."

"If they could call for help, I believe they would have," Mac said.

"Probably, but we're still going there."

Mac knew Ginny's plan wasn't unreasonable, but he hated it all the same. Whoever had sent two men up the mountain to kill him could easily send more, especially if they were pulling from all the people Macklin had ever declined to hire. Still, what she was asking them to do wasn't wrong, so he settled down in the seat and tried not to fidget.

They reached the top of the mountain faster than Mac expected. As the tires of the car crunched on the gravel drive around the station, Mac kept a sharp eye out for movement in or around the building.

The ranger station itself was something of a surprise. Mac realized he'd been expecting another cabin, but the building resembled an old farmhouse, complete with clapboard siding and a long porch with two rocking chairs. In fact, without the large sign declaring it a station, he would have thought Ginny's impeccable sense of direction had failed at last.

Ginny stopped a short distance from the entrance, then shut off the car and reached for her door.

He caught her arm before she could open the door. "You should let me go."

"Why should I do that?" Her tone was so mild that Mac tensed at the sound of it.

"No one seems to be moving around in there, and that's not good."

Ginny opened her mouth to speak, but Mac held up a hand. "We shouldn't take Benji in there until we find out what's happened, so that means someone needs to stay here with him. Someone who can take the car and run if necessary."

"And that someone is me?"

He smiled, hoping to disarm whatever resistance she intended to mount. "You're an excellent driver." He waited while she thought about what he'd said. If there was something bad in there, he was the one to deal with it. He trusted she'd come to the same conclusion if he gave her the space to do it.

At last, she said, "Fine. I'll wait. But be careful."

"I'm always careful."

He approached the building, suspecting that if anyone inside planned to shoot him, they'd have done it as soon as he opened the car door. Sometimes sneaking up on a place simply made one a target for a longer time, so Mac chose the rush-in approach instead. He strode to the porch and climbed the steps without pausing.

The front door opened easily, and he found himself in a relatively narrow entry with a staircase to the second floor straight ahead and rooms on both sides. The walls of the entry hall were lined with bulletin boards and pamphlet racks.

Mac slipped into the first room on the left. The worn hardwood floors were the sole element of hominess left in the place. The rooms were starkly utilitarian with the walls painted a nondescript beige and the furniture cheap and spare. Metal folding tables with folding chairs offered a group work space. Small pressed-wood desks held computers and stacks of paper. Gray metal file cabinets crowded a variety of spaces. The rooms were empty, with none showing signs of a struggle.

The rear of the structure offered two more rooms. One was a kitchen with elderly grayish-beige appliances and an equally elderly wooden table and chairs. A coffeemaker held a pot with a few inches of brown liquid at the bottom. Mac took one whiff of the coffee and wrinkled his nose at the stale smell. Either the rangers made the worst coffee in the world, or it had been left there for a long time.

He crossed to the last downstairs room and found a radio setup. Unlike the others, the radio room showed signs of violence. The radio was badly damaged, likely from the axe on the floor beside it. A scatter of papers lay on the floor next to the table, probably having fallen there when the radio was attacked.

"So much for calling for help from here," he muttered.

He studied the damage and thought he might be able to fix it with enough time, assuming he could find some usable wiring and maybe a soldering iron. Not that it mattered. Driving down the mountain to find help was the wiser option. He didn't want to spend any more time in the eerily silent ranger station than necessary.

Mac squatted to examine the axe but found no traces of blood on it. Apparently the only violence done with it had been to the radio.

So where is everyone?

He checked the stairs next, listening attentively for any sound from the upper rooms. When everything stayed silent, he headed up. The second floor held a bathroom and four small bedrooms, furnished with beds that were barely more than cots, each with a storage chest beside it and hooks on all of the walls, some of which held items of clothing. One of the rooms was messy, but it was the ordinary mess of someone who didn't consider organization to be a top priority.

With nowhere else to search, Mac headed back to the car. He climbed into the passenger seat and told Ginny what he'd found. "There's no blood and no sign of a struggle. The radio is a wreck, but it doesn't appear that anyone tried to stop whoever wrecked it. If the guy killed the rangers, I don't know what he did with them."

"I think I do," Ginny said. "This is good news. It suggests they're still alive and just need a rescue."

Mac was already shaking his head. "We need to get off the mountain. This place is creepy."

"We will get off the mountain," Ginny said. "But I need to check one more place. This time, you stay with Benji. I know where I'm going, and I can get there and back quicker on my own."

Mac hated the sound of that. "Is it far?"

"No. I'll be quick." She was out of the car before he could come up with a decent argument as to why she should stay. He watched her march past the station house with purpose. He was beginning to think the woman was the most courageous person he'd ever met.

He never took his eyes away from the spot where Ginny had disappeared as he began the hardest wait of his life.

Though she could have told Mac where to find the equipment shed, she hadn't wanted another long wait in the car. She much preferred being the one to rush headlong into something.

Even though she moved quickly, Ginny kept a sharp eye on the path, searching for indicators of recent passage, as well as signs of blood or a struggle. So far, nothing. The shed was long and low, built with no thought to making it blend in with the woods or the house that served as the station. The bottom of the shed was clad in some kind of unconvincing rock façade, and the upper half of the walls bore vinyl board-and-batten siding. At one end of the building was a wide double door to allow the vehicles stored inside to be driven in and out.

On the side, a smaller door made an easier entrance for people. Like the one on Alan's shed, it had a large hasp and a shiny padlock. Knowing it was futile but needing to try something anyway, Ginny yanked on the lock, expecting nothing to happen.

Instead she heard several shouts. "Is someone out there? Let us out!"

"Who are you?" she called.

"Park rangers," a man answered. "There are three of us. We were attacked. Who's there?"

Ginny pursed her lips. She had no way of verifying the identity of the rangers. She couldn't exactly ask them to shove their licenses under the door. She had met one park ranger before, so she asked, "Is Ranger Kent Brown in there?"

"I'm here," a second voice called, and Ginny recognized the reedy tenor. "Do I know you?"

"It's Dr. Bryce," she said. "I have a cabin near here."

"I remember you. A man locked us in here. He's dangerous. He has a gun. You need to get out of here in case he returns."

"He won't," Ginny said. "Where is the key to the lock?"

She heard a lower murmur of voices before Ranger Brown called, "We don't know. The gunman had it. But there's a spare in the top drawer of the blue file cabinet in the office."

Ginny didn't respond to that right away. She could go after it if necessary, but she couldn't imagine why the gunman would carry a key to the shed away with him. He wouldn't need it, as it was unlikely that he'd want to come back. If he'd wanted to kill the rangers, he would have done it already.

"Hold on," she said, then began scanning the ground around the shed, kicking at the grass and watching for anything shiny. She slowly widened her search, intending to check everywhere in easy tossing range. She spotted the gleam of metal—the key.

She quickly unlocked the door to the shed, and three rangers burst out. They were in rough shape, dirty and exhausted. The oldest had a split lip, but no one else had any obvious wounds. All three thanked her profusely.

"I'm glad I found you. You should know that the radio in the station is broken," she said.

"Do you have a car?" the man with the split lip asked.

"I do, but I can't loan it to you. I'm heading off the mountain, but I'll send help."

"What if that man comes to tie up loose ends?" asked the third ranger, a middle-aged woman. "He had a gun. He could kill us all."

"He's tied up on the trail that leads here," Ginny said. "If you want to collect him, he should be eager for help, but I would suggest you watch out for a bear. We had an uncomfortably close encounter with one."

The woman's frightened expression grew stony. "We'll keep an eye out."

The older man nodded. "After we get some water. We're pretty dehydrated." He reached out and clasped Ginny's hand. "Thank you again, Dr. Bryce."

"I'm glad you're all right."

Ginny headed for the car, relief having washed away enough worry to make her aware again of how exhausted she was. She'd be glad to be off the mountain. At least with the gunmen handled and the rangers all safe, she, Mac, and Benji had nothing else to worry about.

At least that was what she hoped.

16

They drove down from the mountain, the roads improving steadily from narrow, rutted paths of dirt and gravel to pothole-riddled paved roads, to better and wider options. All the while, Ginny tried to talk herself into releasing some of the tension that had her muscles tight and her head aching. They'd gotten the rangers out of the shed. The gunmen weren't chasing them.

She supposed she should be glad that she wasn't the primary target. After all, if the gunman claimed to have been sent by Mac's company, that meant there was no connection to any of the angry or threatening mail she'd gotten. Once they arrived in the city, she would have escaped the nightmare, but the thought didn't provide the comfort she'd expected.

Did it matter if she was safe, as long as Mac and Benji were in danger? She told herself firmly that the police would be able to protect them. She could go home and put it all behind her. But she found she didn't want to do that. She hated the idea of separating from Mac and Benji.

The realization that she'd broken her cardinal rule and had come to care so much for a patient—and his guardian—filled her with frustration, and she slammed her hand against the steering wheel.

"The car annoying you?" Mac asked, his tone mild.

"No." She suspected he'd keep asking, so she came up with a lame explanation. "I hate leaving without checking out my cabin. We were in such a hurry to get out of there." That was true, at least. She had no idea how badly damaged her cabin was, or what the gunmen had done to it after she fled through the tunnel with Mac and Benji. *Great. All that work to calm me down and all I did was give myself something new to worry about.*

"I'm sure it'll be fine." Mac pulled out his phone. "I've got a signal. Not much of one, but a signal."

"I can do you one better," Ginny said, pointing down the road. "I've got a police car."

Mac jerked his attention to the road ahead. A police car was pulled off to the side of the road on one of the clear areas that frequented the steep roads. Ginny slowed as they approached the law enforcement vehicle, and she could see a young officer through the car window with his cell phone held up to his face. She quickly pulled over and was out of the car almost instantly, eager to speak to the officer. Ginny heard Mac call her name, but she kept moving, almost running toward the car.

The officer climbed out, holding up one hand while the other hovered near his holstered gun. "Stop right there, please."

Ginny stopped, stunned at the officer's reaction. As a well-known psychologist with a mildly imperious nature, she wasn't used to police officers treating her with suspicion, but then she realized all her normal trappings of affluence and normality were gone, except for her nice car. She was simply a dirty, rumpled woman rushing toward the man.

"I'm sorry," she said. "I wasn't thinking. We've been through a lot. We need help. My name is Dr. Virginia Bryce."

"Officer Williams." He continued to watch her with open suspicion.

Then the rear door of Ginny's car opened and Benji hopped out. He trotted over to Ginny and took her hand.

At the sight of the boy, filthy though he was, the officer visibly relaxed, though not completely. Benji smiled up at the officer, almost beaming, and the man relaxed still more. Ginny made a mental promise to give the child the biggest present she could find for helping to calm the nervous officer.

"You guys look like you've had a rough time," the young officer said. "Maybe your husband could get out of the car now too?"

"He's not my husband," Ginny said. "But no problem." She waved at him to join them and Mac climbed out of the car. His movements were easy, but Ginny could see he kept his hands in plain sight. The officer's tension didn't lessen at the sight of Mac, who was easily four or five inches taller than the younger man, but he listened as Ginny and Mac explained what they'd experienced over the last day, and showed the officer their identification. When they reached the end of their abbreviated story, the officer no longer vibrated with nervous tension.

"I'll call this in," the young officer said. "The whole thing is way above my pay grade. You guys will need to stay with me a short while longer."

"Of course," Ginny said. She wished they'd made it to the nearest small town before finding someone to save them. At least then she could have gotten a cup of coffee, and maybe even a hot shower.

While they waited, they answered more questions for the officer as he took careful notes. Though Ginny felt increasingly restless, she was impressed by Mac's relaxed demeanor.

Thankfully Benji took his cues from his uncle rather than her, continuing to gaze around with cheerful interest. Occasionally, he even tugged her hand and pointed out a bird or squirrel, beaming.

To her relief, they didn't wait more than thirty minutes before two more police cars arrived, one of which was unmarked. Immediately after, an ambulance pulled up. While they repeated their story to a detective named Harper, the medical technician from the ambulance cleaned and put fresh bandages on Mac's wound. He also gave them all bottles of water, for which Ginny was truly grateful.

"Excuse me," Detective Harper said when one of the officers called to him. Ginny watched him walk away, curious. She didn't enjoy the feeling that the situation was being taken out of their hands, even though that was exactly what she'd wanted.

The medical technician spoke then. "There's no sign of infection," he told Mac as he smoothed the last piece of tape over the bandage. "You've taken surprisingly good care of this out here."

"That's all Ginny's doing," Mac said. "I probably would have ignored it until my arm fell off."

"Well, you're lucky to have her then," the tech said, sending Ginny a kind smile.

Ginny didn't bother to correct his misunderstanding. It was normal for people to assume that two adults with a child were a couple. And it didn't feel as strange as she'd have thought for people to think that about her and Mac.

She noticed Benji wobbling next to Mac, a mostly-empty water bottle in hand. "I think Benji could use a place to sit down," Ginny said.

The boy blinked at her and rubbed his eyes.

"I'd offer you a gurney," the tech said. "But I'm not sure how much longer I'll be here. It's up to Detective Harper."

"Maybe he could sit in my car again," Ginny said.

"Afraid not," Harper answered as he walked over to them. "I'm going to need to hold onto your car for a while. I've sent people to the ranger station and to find the gunmen you told me about. Until we sort everything out, I'm going to need you to stay close by."

"I understand," Mac said. "But we're nearly dead on our feet. Could we be close by with food in our stomachs and maybe a nap? You have our identification. And if you're holding onto Ginny's car, we can't exactly make a run for it."

Harper inclined his head in acknowledgment of Mac's logic.

"I'll have an officer drive you to a motel. It's pretty much the only place nearby. It's not four-star or anything, but they have a diner. If everything you've said checks out, and I expect it will, you should be able to have your car back by tomorrow or maybe the next day, and then you can head for home."

"That will be great," Mac said.

"Officer Williams will take you to the motel." He directed his next words to the young officer they'd met in the first place. "Tell John the rooms will be taken care of, as well as food."

The ride to the motel passed in a blur, with Ginny fighting the urge to close her burning eyes. She suspected that she'd soon tumble into a deep sleep, and she wanted to be as alert as possible when they reached the hotel. Still, despite her best efforts, she couldn't resist the lure of slumber.

She woke with a jolt when someone gently shook her shoulder. Mac was leaning on the door of the police car, which was parked in front of a long strip of motel rooms. At one end, a small diner sported faded paint and a sign that advertised "tasty" food.

She rubbed at her face. "How's Benji?"

"Perkier than either of us," Mac said. He pointed toward the walkway in front of the nearest room, where Benji jumped back and forth over a crack. "Officer Williams is in the office getting our room keys."

"They do know we need more than one, right?" she asked, suddenly not sure if she'd mentioned that to the police officer.

"They know," Mac assured her.

Ginny swung her legs around and got out of the car smoothly, for which she was grateful. She still felt slow and tired, though maybe a little better than before. She stood and stretched. "I could sleep for a week."

"That sounds great," Mac said. "Though I need food first."

"I need a shower first. I hope the water here is hot."

Mac waved a hand toward the motel office. "I guess we're about to find out."

The room couldn't be considered spacious, but it smelled freshly cleaned and had two double beds. It was all Mac could do not to collapse onto one of them, but the ache of hunger kept that from being a priority. He considered the shower Ginny had mentioned but decided he needed food more urgently. Food and phone calls.

The sound of springs pulled his attention toward Benji, who was bouncing on the second bed. Mac was delighted to see Benji doing a normal kid thing. Though the boy was still not talking, he struck Mac as better than before they'd come to see Ginny. He was more connected, less inclined to sit and stare.

A run from gunmen through the woods was a strange sort of therapy, Mac reflected. He set his phone down on a cheap pressed-wood table and headed into the bathroom. He wouldn't take the time for a shower, but some cold water splashed on his face would help.

The mirror in the bathroom revealed a man in need of a shave and sleep. Dark shadows pooled under his eyes, and he saw a long scratch running down one cheek that he hadn't even realized he had. No wonder the police officers had gaped at him while he'd told his story. He must have looked like a distraught hiker wandering out of the woods.

He splashed water on his face, then grabbed a thin washcloth from the pile on a metal shelf. He soaped it up and used it to clean away dirt and dried blood from as much of his skin as he could easily reach. His clothes still needed washing, but at least he wouldn't scare folks anymore.

"Benji?" he called. "Come here and let's get you washed up."

The boy reluctantly shuffled into the bathroom. He grimaced but stood still as Mac washed his face with another of the thin washcloths and made some attempt to tame the boy's hair. He pulled the sweater they'd gotten from the lawyer's cabin over Benji's head and saw that the sweatshirt underneath was far cleaner than anything Mac wore.

"I believe you'll be the most presentable one in our group," he said. "I need to make some phone calls, then we can eat, okay?"

Benji's eyes lit up at the idea of food, and Mac felt guilty. He was supposed to take care of the boy, and instead, he'd dragged him all over a mountain without even the basic necessities. It was high time to right that wrong. "I'll be quick," Mac promised.

He left the bathroom and took his phone over to sit on one of the beds. Cal should still be in the office. Mac could call and tell his friend and business partner about everything they'd experienced. Cal would be the best one to track down who had been digging through the records of past applicants.

Still, something kept Mac from making that call. He trusted Cal. They'd known each other since the younger man had been a small boy, racing tricycles up and down the sidewalk with Derrick. The two boys had been inseparable, constantly trying to keep up with the older Mac. Mac was the one who'd taught them both how to ride two-wheelers and how to play baseball, though they'd never taken to the sport the way Mac had.

It was ridiculous not to trust Cal, but somehow Mac couldn't quite force himself to dial the number. Someone had hired men that Macklin Security had passed over. Someone had given them the job of tracking down Mac and killing him. That same person hadn't cared to do anything to protect Ginny and Benji. Whoever it was could have the office under surveillance, could have Cal under surveillance.

If Mac called Cal and told him what happened, told him where they were, he trusted that Cal wouldn't pass on the information. But he also knew Cal had no poker face. When he heard about Mac and Benji's close call, he'd be panicked and upset. Anyone watching would know that, and it could make Cal a target too. Mac couldn't let that happen.

When Ginny's car was released and they made it back to the city, Mac would go directly to the office and do his own digging. And he would impress on Cal the danger he might be in. Once he was in the city, Mac stood a better chance of keeping the younger man safe. That would be the best plan for all of them. For now, they could eat and rest. He felt a weight lift as he made the decision, something he took as a sign that he'd made the right choice.

Mac stood and shoved the phone into his pocket. Benji had returned to bouncing gently on the other bed, but he leaped to his feet in an instant, his eyes hopeful. "How about we go see if that diner has good fries?" The words were barely out of Mac's mouth before his stomach growled loudly.

To his astonishment, Benji laughed.

The sound was so easy that it was as if nearly two months hadn't passed since the last time the boy had made it, and Mac had to blink away tears. Whatever happened next, at the moment they were all right, and that counted for a lot.

He held out a hand, and Benji slipped his own into it. Together they headed out of the room into the afternoon sunlight that filtered through trees all around them. They might be in a motel with a short strip mall across the street, but the woods peeked at them from all around, as if waiting to reclaim the tiny patch of civilization.

Benji tugged on Mac's hand, not interested in enjoying the mountain air or the scenery. The door to the room beside theirs opened and Ginny stepped out. Benji let go of Mac's hand and raced over to her. He threw his arms around her legs, and she laughed and hugged him back.

"You cleaned up," she said to him. "You're very handsome."

Benji pointed toward the diner.

Ginny grinned. "Great minds think alike. I was on my way to find a really big salad."

Benji wrinkled his nose.

"Benji and I were thinking more along the lines of a burger and fries," Mac said.

"Of course you were," Ginny said, rolling her eyes. "I think I'll stick with salad." She tipped a mischievous wink to Benji. "That way I'll have room for pie."

Benji took Ginny's hand and towed her toward the diner. Mac fell in beside them. It felt natural to walk together that way, and Mac felt some of the tension ease from him. *Relax. We beat the bad guys. We're all fine. It's all easy from now on.*

If only he could make himself believe it.

17

The next morning, Detective Harper found Mac, Ginny, and Benji having breakfast in the diner. He stood next to their chipped Formica-topped table, and his eyes swept over Mac's blue T-shirt with cartoon ponies on it. Harper's eyebrows rose, but Mac ignored the implied question. Let the man think what he would.

The truth was that Ginny had walked across the street to a thrift shop in the small strip mall. She'd picked up sweats and T-shirts for each of them to sleep in, and a change of clothes for Benji for the next day as well. When she'd handed over the clothes, she apologized, saying she hadn't even tried to guess at Mac's jeans size when looking for clothes for the drive home. *"The number of T-shirts was more limited than I expected too."*

He'd told her not to worry about it and thanked her for her thoughtfulness. Though neither the pony shirt nor the one with the grumpy pig that he'd worn to bed were exactly his style, the ridiculousness of the ponies had made him laugh when he'd pulled the shirt on after his morning shower. He appreciated having even that small thing to laugh at.

He waited to see if Harper would waste an actual question on it. The man did not. Instead, he rocked on his heels and said, "Sorry to interrupt your breakfast, folks."

"It's not a problem," Ginny said. "Would you care to join us, Detective? We have room."

Mac expected him to refuse, but Harper's attention wandered to Benji, who eyed him with friendly curiosity. "Thank you. I'd enjoy that."

He took a seat beside Mac and smiled at Benji. "I have a son your age," he said. "His name is Jack. He loves dinosaurs. I assume you do too?" Harper pointed at the trio of plastic dinosaurs Ginny had found at the thrift store and bought for Benji.

Benji nodded.

"Do you have a favorite?"

The boy held up a T. rex, the plastic figure caught in the middle of an open-mouthed roar.

"That one would be mine too," Harper said. "Jack's is the diplodocus, but I think he likes the sound of the name more than anything." He paused as a waitress bustled over to fill a cup with coffee for him and wish him a good morning.

Harper returned the greeting but didn't speak again until the waitress was well away from the table. He gazed at Mac, dark eyes amused. "We found the man who attacked the park rangers, exactly where you said he was."

Mac took a bite of his toast without comment.

"The guy kept demanding to be taken to the hospital to be treated for a snakebite, but the emergency techs said he hadn't been bitten. It was clear he'd seen some rough road though."

"He deserved worse," Ginny said coldly.

"I don't doubt it. He confirmed your account that he'd been hired by Macklin Security, though he says he was never trying to kill you, only to detain you." Ginny straightened abruptly and opened her mouth, but the detective held up a hand. "We have more than enough evidence to prove he and his partner were trying to kill you."

"Did he happen to remember the name of whoever hired him?" Mac asked.

"No, and he insisted that he never went to the actual office of Macklin Security after his initial attempt to get a job there. The story is so fishy it stinks, but I'm inclined to think the guy believes it."

Mac had to agree. "I got that feeling too."

Detective Harper gestured to a plate in the center of the table that held a pile of toast. "Do you mind?"

"Help yourself," Ginny answered.

The man selected a piece and slathered it thickly with strawberry jam. "We also found the partner. It seems he had a run-in with a bear."

"We thought he had. That must have been unpleasant," Ginny said.

"You've got that right." He bit into the toast and the crunch sounded loud at the quiet table.

"I had an encounter with that particular bear too," Mac said, holding up his bandaged arm. "Thankfully, I made it out alive."

Harper didn't comment on that. "Since everything we've seen supports your story, you are all free to go. Unfortunately, your cars are still being processed, as is your cabin, and I can't imagine the SUV is drivable anyway. I can give you a lift to a car rental agency if you want."

"When will I be able to return to my cabin?" Ginny asked.

The detective winced. "Could be a couple days. This is not the sort of situation we deal with regularly around here, so we're going to take care to do it right. But I have your contact information in the city, and I can let you know when we're done."

Though she pressed her lips together into a fine line, she didn't argue.

Harper pulled a card out of his pocket. "I've jotted down the name of a police detective in New York City. I happen to know him, so he's assisting. The exciting part may have gone down in the woods here, but it's clear to us it originated there. If you want to get updates from someone local, he'll be a good option."

Ginny took the card and shoved it into the pocket of her jacket.

"We'll accept the ride to the car rental gratefully," Mac said. "I'm sure we're all eager to go home."

They didn't immediately leave the diner, but the conversation shifted to something more pleasant as they finished eating. They learned that Harper loved his home and was passionate about the area. Mac was almost inclined to tell the man that it didn't matter how good the fishing was in the local lake since he intended never to return after their experience in the woods, but he saw the way Benji hung on the man's every word, so he kept his opinions to himself.

When they were finally on the road to the city, with Mac driving, Benji marched his dinosaurs around in the back seat, an activity so common and innocent that it squeezed Mac's heart every time he glanced into the rearview mirror.

"Ginny," Mac said, speaking quietly with the hope Benji wasn't listening. "Can Benji spend some time with you once we get to the city? I have to find out who is after me. I don't want to put him in any more danger."

"I'd love that," Ginny said. "But there's something I'm going to have to do first. Last night I tried to get in touch with my assistant, Willow Reed. I'm always able to get through to Willow, but she's not answering. Considering what we've been through over the last few days, I'm worried."

"I can't imagine it could be connected with what's happened to us," Mac said, frowning.

"Probably not," Ginny agreed. "But until I go to her apartment to see her and learn why she hasn't been answering my calls, I won't be sure I'm any safer than you."

Inwardly Mac chafed at any delay in getting to Macklin Security and finding out exactly what was going on, but he could see Ginny's point. And she'd done more than enough to earn his agreement. "No problem. We can go to your assistant's apartment together."

"All three of us?" Ginny asked. "If something dangerous is going on, I'm absolutely not willing to do that."

"No, not all three of us." Mac wasn't thrilled with what he was about to say, but he knew it was the best course of action for them. "I do have one completely safe place that Benji could spend a few hours, though not more than that."

"Oh?" Ginny said, the questioning tone suggesting she hoped for more explanation, but Mac didn't provide it, and she didn't push. The answer would be tough to explain, and Ginny would understand once they were there.

"Benji?" Mac said, raising his voice to get his nephew's attention. The boy's eyes met his in the mirror. "We're going to stop by Uncle Bill's apartment. That okay with you?"

Benji gave a hop of excitement in his seat. Mac agreed. Mac's uncle Bill was the kind of guy kids loved and moms fretted about. A retired cop, Bill made miniatures as a hobby and a tidy boost to his retirement income. The fact that they were tiny scenes of famous murders tended to make Benji's mom come up with reasons why Benji should limit his time there. She'd worried they would give the boy nightmares. The irony of that being the safest place for Benji in light of everything the boy had been through wasn't lost on Mac.

But he couldn't see any other way.

18

When Bill opened the door, his face lit up. "Well, hello there."

"Hey, Bill. Sorry I didn't call first," Mac said. "My phone is dead."

"Don't worry about it," Bill said heartily as he ushered them into his apartment. The home was old with small rooms and worn furniture, but Bill kept it surprisingly clean. Signs of his hobby were in evidence everywhere, such as a rack holding sheets of basswood and balsa, waiting to be cut up and transformed into the boxes for the vignettes or tiny furniture to go inside each scene.

"It's about time Mac brought a lady friend around," Bill announced, much to Mac's chagrin, but Ginny was gracious and friendly to the older man, showing no sign of discomfort with Bill's bluntness.

"What is that you're wearing?" Bill demanded, pointing to the part of Mac's T-shirt that was visible under his leather jacket.

"A thrift shop find," Mac said, then grinned. "Don't you like it?"

"It's weirder than any of the miniatures I've made," the older man said.

"Ginny gave it to me."

Bill spun to gape at Ginny's innocent face, then shook his head. "Must be love, then, to get my nephew to wear that."

Ginny laughed. "I think it was simply limited choices and desperation for a clean shirt." She deftly avoided further conversation on the topic of her and Mac by asking about a table where a freestanding magnifying glass helped Bill paint his intricate figures. "Who are you making over here?"

"Jack the Ripper," Bill said with obvious glee. "You'd be surprised by how many times I've done him. People never get tired of him. It's my most popular diorama."

Ginny gave him a completely deadpan expression and said, "People are interesting."

Before his uncle could work out what she meant, Mac cut in. "Bill, can Benji stay here for a couple hours? I know it's short notice, but I need to do something that I can't really talk about, and it's not safe to take him with me."

Benji peered into Mac's face, his eyes narrowed with suspicion. He left the scene he'd been examining, shifted all his dinosaurs to the crook of one arm, and took Ginny's hand. The message was clear. He wanted to stay with her.

"I'll come and get you in a couple hours, maybe less," she said. "But I have to go check on someone. Besides, my apartment isn't nearly as cool as this one."

Benji considered that, then let go of Ginny's hand and hopped onto a well-worn recliner, marching the dinosaurs along the arms.

"You're good to go," Bill said. "I don't know what's up here, but I hope there will be time for a long explanation later. Until then, Benji will be safe here until I see you again."

"Thanks, Bill." Impulsively Mac gave his uncle a hug, surprising the older man and probably worrying him more than he already was.

Bill scowled at them. "You stay safe, you hear?"

"Yes sir," Mac agreed, with a silent prayer that he'd be able to keep the promise.

The drive to Willow's apartment building was almost completely silent as Ginny's thoughts swung between worry about her assistant and wonder at how dramatically her life had changed in such a short time. Neither was something she wanted to dwell on, so her thoughts rotated, as she'd push out one subject only to have another rush in.

She had taken over driving since she was more familiar with the streets around Willow's apartment building. Mac seemed content to leave her in peace with her thoughts, though she was aware of his eyes on her. She didn't know what to say to him. It was the first time they'd been together without Benji nearby, and she felt off balance, almost shy. It wasn't a sensation she was used to and so she swallowed it down, letting her worry for Willow pop into its place.

"Willow's apartment is right up here," she said. "All I have to do is find a place to park."

Mac actually laughed. "Yeah, because that's so easy in New York."

She gave him a grin. "I know. Maybe we'll be lucky."

It didn't take nearly as long as either of them had expected, and the hike to the front of the apartment building from the spot she found wasn't far either. Maybe things really were looking up. Still, it was all she could do not to break into a run as she hurried to Willow's apartment building, dodging between others on the sidewalk. Even the normal New Yorker pace was too slow for Ginny's nerves.

When they reached the door and pushed the button, someone buzzed them in without even speaking. "That's not safe," Ginny muttered as she swung the door open.

Mac caught her arm before she could rush in. "Unless you're right and something is not normal here. Maybe someone wants us up there."

"It doesn't matter," Ginny insisted. "I have to see if Willow's okay."

Mac didn't argue, but when they reached the top of the stairs in front of Willow's apartment, he insisted on standing in front of Ginny. "I'm a better shield, and one of us has to get back to Benji."

She didn't have an argument for that, so she let him knock.

They stood without a sound, but no one answered the door. Mac rapped on the door again. "I'm not impressed with that door," he said. "If she doesn't answer, I think I can knock it down."

Willow wouldn't thank her for that if she was okay, but Ginny found she didn't much care. She gestured for him to go ahead. Mac took a couple of steps back, apparently preparing to kick the door down, but then it swung open.

An extremely rumpled young woman stood in the doorway, blinking at them. "What on earth?" Willow demanded.

"What's wrong with you?" Ginny snapped. "Why haven't you answered my calls?"

Willow moaned and put her hands over her ears. "Don't yell at me. My head hurts. You can come in if you're not going to shout anymore."

Ginny followed her inside. "Willow," she said, her voice so quiet, it was almost a whisper. "Where have you been?"

"My sister's wedding," Willow said, shuffling into the tiny kitchenette as she spoke. She picked up a cup of coffee. "I've been talking about it for weeks. I had to switch off my phone for the wedding, and I guess I forgot about it. It was a great reception. I had to stay over at my Mom's because I wasn't fit to drive."

"I was worried."

"You were out in the boonies with no telephone reception," Willow said. "I had no way of knowing you'd try to call me. You said you'd be unavailable for weeks." Then she squinted at Mac, nearsighted without the glasses she usually wore. "Apparently you changed your plans."

Ginny found Willow's speculative expression annoying. Why did everyone assume she and Mac were a couple? It wasn't as if she had no male colleagues. Mac didn't resemble any of the psychologists Ginny knew, but that didn't mean he couldn't be one.

Not wanting to hold him up any longer, despite how patiently he waited, she squared her shoulders and faced him. "I'll go pick up Benji now. Actually, I'll pick up some groceries and then get him. Benji could use some decent food—something that's never been in a can or fried."

"He'll be thrilled," Mac said dryly.

"He'll love it. I'm an excellent cook."

"I don't doubt it. Thanks for taking care of him. I'll come by as soon as I'm sure it's safe." Then he stopped and blinked. "Um, I don't know where you live."

Ginny heard Willow giggle and had to suppress the urge to glare at the girl. Instead, she gave Mac her address and told him the bellman would be expecting him. Then she said, "I can go with you if you want. Benji is in safe hands, and you shouldn't do this alone. I could help."

Mac didn't reply at first, and Ginny could almost sense his amusement at the thought of her being any kind of backup. The suspicion annoyed her. He ought to be aware of what she could do by that point.

"Thank you," he said. "I don't want to put you in any further danger. I'll call as soon as I know anything."

"Fine." Ginny held out the car keys.

Mac waved them off. "I'll call a cab. You keep the car since you're going to have Benji."

With nothing left to say, but not happy about his leaving to confront some unknown danger alone, Ginny walked him to the door of Willow's apartment. "Be careful."

"Always." Then he shocked Ginny by leaning forward quickly and kissing her on the cheek. It was a fond gesture, something a brother might do, but somehow it didn't feel brotherly when matched with the gleam in Mac's eyes. But before Ginny could come up with words of any sort, he was gone.

"Well, he's gorgeous," Willow said. "Did you find him out in the woods?"

"In a manner of speaking." She folded her arms over her chest. "You should probably take some aspirin and go to bed. I've got errands to run."

"You mean you aren't going to tell me about that guy? The one you didn't even introduce me to. And what was all that talk about danger?"

"Never mind. You remember that you work for me, right?" Ginny said. "Where is your usual professional tone?"

"Lost in the headache," Willow said. "Plus, my mom says you should treat me better. I'm an excellent assistant, and we're not all that easy to find."

Ginny appraised her thoughtfully. "You might be right about that."

"Besides, you were worried about me." Willow gave her boss a cheeky grin. "So you care."

"I care about all sorts of things," Ginny said. "Now I have to get going."

"One more thing," Willow said. "You got a notification after you'd already left for your woodland retreat. The Jenkins boy has been returned to his family."

"Really?" Ginny asked. "That's great. I felt terrible that I couldn't keep them from being separated."

"Yeah, the parents felt terrible too. I could tell by all the hate mail they sent you. But now you should get a lot less. That's good news."

"I'm not worried about hate mail," Ginny said. "But if the family is together and stable again, that's wonderful news. Sometimes it's hard to hope for a happy ending." She found she appreciated the idea of even a small hope.

"You can add the Jenkins family to your other good news," Willow said.

"Other good news?"

"That your long, sad, lonely streak is over. And talk about a comeback. That guy is seriously A-list."

Ginny considered explaining that she wasn't dating Mac, but that would lead to questions she did not have time to answer, so she settled for the simple truth. "Yes, he is."

19

Mac hadn't even reached the sidewalk before he began to miss Ginny. Bringing her with him would have been ridiculous and wrong. She was safe now and didn't need to be dragged any farther into whatever was happening in his life. Still, it took more effort than he cared to admit to leave her behind.

He had to focus, but though he tried to as the cab carried him to Macklin Security, something kept him wallowing in guilt for leaving Ginny and Benji.

The last time I left them for their own good, up on the mountain, things didn't go so well, did they?

Mac shoved the question down. He wasn't on the mountain anymore, and Bill was perfectly capable of keeping Benji safe. Besides, Ginny had taken care of herself and his nephew. She was far from a damsel in distress.

"Hey!" the cabdriver half yelled. "We're here."

Mac got out of the car and paid the driver, grateful that with all the stuff he'd left behind in his SUV, he still had his wallet. He strode across the sidewalk toward the building, refusing to let fear seep in. Sure, whoever wanted to kill him might be watching Macklin Security, but they could be anywhere. He wasn't going to cower. That wasn't what Macklins did.

When he walked into the entry, the building receptionist, Caitlin, beamed at him. The second he saw her expression, his brother's voice rang in his memory, teasing Mac about how Caitlin had a crush on him.

He had slugged Derrick playfully in the arm and reminded him they weren't in high school. Grown women didn't have crushes.

"Sure they don't," Derrick had said, laughing. "I'm telling you, brother, you need to ask Caitlin out. One night listening to you make awkward conversation over dinner would cure her completely."

Mac had never done as his brother suggested, and the receptionist continued to glow every time he went into the office. "Are you returning to work any time soon?" Caitlin asked.

"Not yet," Mac said. "This is a special visit. Is Cal in? Have you seen him?"

"I think so," she said, showing she wasn't nearly as attentive to Cal's coming and going as she was to his. Mac almost chuckled. As usual, his little brother was probably right.

"Thanks." Mac headed for the elevator that would take him to the fourth floor, where Macklin Security occupied most of the office space. There was a bail bondsman in the small office that took up the rest of the floor, but Mac rarely saw the man. When he did, the bail bondsman had the worn-out appearance of someone who'd worked too long at a job that didn't bring him joy.

The door to the office of Macklin Security was beautiful, unmarred mahogany. The sign identifying the company had been painted directly on the wall beside the door in blue, Derrick's favorite color. Derrick had insisted that blue was the color of competence and calm. Mac didn't care one way or the other, but he approved of the result with the clear block lettering and the way the stylized *M* resembled an eye. The logo eye checked out each person who came to their office.

He tapped the eye. *You should have been paying more attention lately.* Mac quickly zipped up his jacket to hide the ponies on his shirt, then squared his shoulders. There were answers inside. There had to be.

The door opened easily under Mac's hand, though it felt strange to step through it. He'd rarely been in the office since Derrick died. Benji needed his time far more than the company. His passion for the work he'd done there had waned with the absence of Derrick himself.

The reception desk was empty of the older woman, Ellen, who usually sat there, but Cal was next to it, flipping through envelopes. The younger man wore what Mac had come to think of as his uniform—jeans and one of the company's T-shirts. It was the same thing many of their bodyguards wore when the job called for casual clothes, but for Cal, it was simply a comfortable choice that also reflected the company.

Cal did a double take when he raised his head. "Mac?" The surprise melted into a crooked grin. "Are you here to work?"

"Something like that," Mac said.

"How's Benji?" Cal asked as he circled the desk to sit on the front corner near Mac.

"He's doing surprisingly well, all things considered. Tell me, have you seen any sign of suspicious activity lately? Have any of our people shown an interest in information about the company that's none of their business?"

"What kind of information?"

"Information about who has applied for a job recently and been passed over."

Cal's forehead wrinkled. "I don't think so."

"Well, someone has recently obtained exactly that information. So if it's not one of the people we employ, then someone has hacked into our system to find it."

"That's not possible. Our cybersecurity is state of the art. It has to be. As you well know, some of our clients have secrets."

"Unfortunately, I've had to expand my view on what is or isn't possible. While Benji and I were visiting that psychologist I told you about, we were attacked."

"Attacked!"

"Shot at, by two gunmen. I managed to have a chat with one of them, eventually, and he said he'd applied for a job right here. He'd been passed over."

"A lot of applicants are," Cal said. "Not everyone can win the kind of trust we need to have in our employees."

Mac didn't need a lesson on how his business worked, but sometimes Cal enjoyed the sound of his own voice. "The guy said he was contacted and offered a job with the company—if he agreed to take out a couple of terrorists. The alleged terrorists were me and the psychologist I'd gone to consult with. The guy said he didn't intend to hurt Benji, but considering the two gunmen opened fire on a cabin with Benji inside, I'm inclined to doubt his word."

Cal sucked air through his teeth. "But Benji is all right?"

"He's fine. So is the psychologist, and the only real damage I took was from a bear, rather than the gunmen. Neither man will be coming after us again, but whoever sent them may simply try something different. That means we need to find how our security was breached, and by whom."

"I'll do everything I can," Cal assured Mac. "Where should we start?"

When Ginny tapped at Bill's door, the older man called, "Hold on a minute. I'm coming."

He opened the door a crack and peered at her past the security chain, then slid it away to let her in. "You were quick. Benji didn't even have time to toss the place." He laughed at his own joke, and Ginny found the sound contagious. She chuckled, despite how worried she still felt about Mac.

"I was going to stop for some groceries," she said. "But I realized I should probably take Benji along so he can show me what he likes to eat."

"He's a kid. He wants sugar in all its many forms." Bill shuffled toward the chair where Benji sat drawing with his dinosaurs peering down at the art from the chair arms. "I guess our time is up, champ."

Benji waved at Ginny, then pushed the pad aside to gather up his dinosaurs. Bill caught the pad before it could hit the floor and examined the drawing Benji had done. "This guy is scary," he said. "He could fit into one of my dioramas."

Ginny stepped closer and saw that the drawing was the same monster Benji had created so many times. Then she noticed something she hadn't seen before. She took the pad from Bill and stared at the sketch. In many ways, it was the same picture she'd seen over and over. The drawing was a composition of dark pencil scribbles, a human-like figure with huge, round, blank eyes, and a black hole for a mouth. Benji had drawn the creature's chest, its arms sticking out from the sides.

The difference from earlier drawings was the lines that bisected the creature's arms and the semicircle that separated the top of the body from the head. She knew immediately what Benji had indicated with the lines. It wasn't the monster's bare body. It was a shirt. A T-shirt with a staring eye in the middle of it.

Suddenly, she understood that the eye wasn't meant to be growing out of the chest of the monster but was instead printed on a shirt.

She recognized that oddly shaped eye, and the recognition froze her to her core.

The stylized eye made up the emblem for Macklin Security. It was printed on the business card Mac had given her.

The scary man in Benji's drawing wore a shirt bearing the logo for Macklin Security.

Considering one of the men who'd tried to kill them in the mountains claimed to have been sent by Macklin, the fact that Benji's monster wore a Macklin Security T-shirt—and apparently had all along—was staggering. Then she thought of Mac's description of his partner, Cal. What had Mac said—something about how Cal looked like a kid in his T-shirts and thick glasses? Did Cal's glasses make his eyes appear bigger, rounder?

The man Mac trusted completely, the one he considered family, was the scary man in Benji's drawing. Ginny held the paper up toward Benji. "Is this Cal?"

Benji's eyes widened in alarm. He raised his finger to his lips to silence her.

She swallowed hard. "Bill," she said, her voice tight with strain. "Can Benji stay here a while longer? I need to run one more errand."

"No problem," Bill said. "Benji's always good company. You okay, Doc?"

"I'm fine. Everything's fine." She forced a smile as she handed the pad to Benji. "I'll see you soon."

Benji bobbed his head, but his eyes stayed wide and frightened, much as they had when she first met him. She didn't bother telling him it was going to be okay. She had no way to ensure that was true, but she would do absolutely everything in her power to see that it would be.

With that, she left Bill's apartment and sprinted for her car, praying she wasn't too late.

20

In the Macklin Security office, Cal dogged Mac's every step, peppering him with questions. "I can't believe you left Benji to come here. Are you sure he's safe?"

"I left him with my uncle Bill," Mac said as he leafed through files in one of the tall metal cabinets.

Cal laughed. "Benji's mom would be furious."

"Madison always worried that Bill's hobby would give Benji nightmares." Mac wished they had the luxury of worrying about something so insignificant. Benji did have nightmares. He'd had one in the hotel the night before, even. But they weren't about anything as harmless as Bill's miniature creations.

"I've never seen any of Bill's dioramas," Cal said. "They sound cool. But if someone is after you, are you sure an old man can protect the boy?"

Mac stopped flipping through the file folders, knowing he was giving the task half his attention. "My uncle is retired, but he hasn't slowed down much. He's still got some solid cop instincts. Besides, why would someone go after a child? I'm assuming it's me they want, though I can't think of a reason why anyone would."

"Man, I'm so sorry about all this. I know you were trying to get Benji to a therapist. He's going to need one twice as badly now."

"He's got one," Mac said. The one thing he felt extremely confident about was Ginny's presence in Benji's life. He'd seen her concern for Benji and knew she wouldn't give up on the child. He pointed into the drawer. "You want to tell me where the file of applicants is?"

Cal stepped closer and plucked out the right folder. "Here. You'd almost gotten to it. Shouldn't give up so easily."

"I wouldn't have if someone weren't talking my ear off," Mac grumbled, snatching the folder from his hand.

"Hey," Cal complained. "I'm concerned. I would have been the kid's godfather if nepotism hadn't won out over lifelong friendship."

"I'm not sure it was nepotism." Mac crossed to the nearest desk and dropped into a chair. "Madison was afraid you'd pass along your gaming addiction."

"We all have our hobbies. Derrick loved heading out into the woods and sleeping under the stars. Your uncle Bill is obsessed with those historically accurate dioramas. And I enjoy defeating zombies on my computer." He cocked his head to peer at Mac. "You know, I have no idea what your hobby is."

Mac paused shuffling through the applications, frustrated that so few of them included photos. He gave Cal's comment some thought. "Sports, probably."

"Oh, right. Hey, there are some great sports video games. We could play sometime."

Mac didn't even respond to that, though he realized Cal might be missing Derrick too. Mac had left Cal to handle everything when the younger man was probably still grieving. After all, Cal and Derrick had been so close. Mac made a mental note to do more to reconnect with his remaining partner, as soon as he found out who was trying to kill him and Benji. It was time for all of them to move forward.

He'd flipped through every page in the file, but none of the applications that included photos showed either of the gunmen from the woods. Either the gunmen were among the files without photos—in which case Mac doubted he could guess which of the applicants had tried to kill him—or the gunmen's files had been removed.

"I don't suppose Benji is talking yet?"

Mac was still staring into the files and simply shook his head. "No, but I think he's more alert." He thought of Benji slipping his hand into Ginny's or playing with the dinosaurs Ginny had bought him. His nephew had been clammed up inside himself since the accident, but he was doing better now. "If Ginny keeps working with him, he'll be fine. He'll talk again. As weird as it is, even after all we've been through, I have more hope now."

"That's good," Cal said. "As long as it isn't wishful thinking."

Mac grunted. "Wishful thinking can get a guy through sometimes." He tossed the folder on the desk. "I have no way of telling which of those guys came after us. It wasn't one of the applications with a photo. But I still have to consider the possibility that someone got into our computers. I assume all the information on each of these is also in our system."

"Yeah," Cal said. "Paper is great, but I'm always happiest when I can find things with a few keystrokes. I digitize everything."

"Then we need to check for signs of incursion."

"By 'we,' I assume you mean me," Cal said.

"You are the computer guy."

Cal cracked his knuckles. "That I am." He dropped into a chair at a nearby desk and booted up the computer. "And I'm good. Which is how I know no one got into our system without my knowledge."

"Someone knew who we've rejected for jobs," Mac said. "We have to find out who. There's no other way to put an end to this."

"I'll do anything I can," Cal assured him. "I want this to be over too. And not just because it's making me look bad, to say nothing of the company."

Mac wiggled the mouse to wake up the computer in front of him and logged on. He found and selected a file titled *Rejected Applicants*.

"If you're going to race me to find out what happened," Cal said, "I'm telling you right now that you might as well give that up."

"No, I'm going to compare the electronic files to the paper files," Mac said.

"What will that prove?" Cal asked.

"I don't know." Mac struck the desk in frustration. "I'm flailing around. I know what. Did anyone, at any time, ask you anything about our hiring practices?"

"I would have mentioned that," Cal said. "I'm not going to forget some mysterious evildoer quizzing me about our hiring practices. Maybe the guy who shot at you was lying. Crooks do that, I understand."

"That's possible," Mac admitted. "But the guy was scared."

"All the more reason to tell you anything he could think of, whether it was true or not."

"Maybe." Mac continued to click through the Rejected Applicants file. The Macklin Security computer files were always well organized and maintained. Mac had never had a complaint about Cal's work. The guy was meticulous.

One by one, Mac compared scans of the applications to the actual paper copies in his hand. He discovered that sometimes there were scans of photos, even when there was no print photo in the paper file. He asked Cal why that was.

"Sometimes people email their photo after they've been interviewed," Cal said. "That happens when we're seriously considering them, but they didn't think to include a photo. It's rare you'll find that in the rejected files because we would normally hire the person if we're that interested."

"I see." He stared into the eyes of a man on the screen. He wasn't either of the two gunmen from up in the mountains, but if a photo could exist for him, it could potentially exist for others. He sat up straighter, hopeful again.

He'd gone through three more files before he found another that contained a scanned photo when the print file had none. He opened it and found himself face-to-face with the man who had sat in a ball of misery on the mountain trail, telling Mac that his own company had sent someone to kill him. For an instant, Mac was frozen, caught up in how normal the man appeared. None of the exhaustion and desperation that had shown on his face the last time Mac saw him.

"Cal," he said. "I found one of the gunmen. His name is Griffin Suttles. Does that name ring a bell?" He raised his head to peek over the top of the computer monitor, expecting to find Cal watching him from behind the other computer. But Cal wasn't at his computer.

For most of Mac's life, he'd thought of Cal as a friendly kid, though none of them had been children for decades. None of that open friendliness showed on Cal's face anymore. Instead, his brother's best friend glared at Mac with cold, determined eyes. But that was the least menacing part of what Mac saw.

Cal held a gun—the same firearm that was normally stored in a locked box in the office—pointed directly at Mac. The hand that held the weapon didn't shake. Mac realized he should have seen it coming, but he'd believed Cal was family. He couldn't wrap his mind around the idea of Cal's betrayal. Against his better judgment, Mac had pushed aside logic that had pointed to Cal as the most likely person at Macklin Security to have hired formerly rejected applicants.

And sent those same gunmen into the mountains after him and Benji.

The office building that housed Macklin Security had an attached parking garage, so Ginny had no problem finding a place to park.

Fighting panic, she dashed from the parking garage to the building's front door, then slowed when she saw someone sitting at the building's reception desk. It wouldn't do to burst in making demands. They would likely deny her entry if she did.

She swallowed her worry and pushed the glass door open, pulling on her normal professional demeanor like a suit jacket. She was far less put together than usual, but Ginny didn't doubt her attitude would make up for any shortfall in her appearance. "Good morning," she said to the receptionist. "Has Joseph Macklin come through here?"

The woman studied Ginny, her expression pleasant but cool. "I don't normally report on our clients' comings and goings."

"That's reasonable," Ginny replied, her tone implacable. "Are Cal and Mac in the office right now?"

The woman's expression grew cooler. "I'm not in the habit of reporting—"

Ginny held up a hand to stop the repetition. "I need to call the police detective who's handling a case involving an attack on Mac. I want to give him accurate information. Since you can't talk to me, I assume I can simply hand you the phone once I have him on the line. And with any luck, the delay from your obstruction won't result in any harm to Mac."

"There's no need to be rude," the woman snapped. "Mac and Cal are both in the office. I wouldn't bet on anyone who might be planning to attack them. They are in security after all."

"Good to know. Where is their office?"

"Fourth floor. You can't miss it."

"Thank you," Ginny said and started toward the elevators.

"I thought you were calling the police," the receptionist said, her tone thick with suspicion.

Ginny realized she would probably call upstairs if Ginny got in the elevator. Since that would be as sure to tip off Cal as Mac, she couldn't risk it. Instead, she turned back to the reception desk again, though she chafed at the delay.

"I am." Ginny retrieved the card Detective Harper had given her back in the mountains. She called the number and was mildly surprised to be put through to the NYPD detective—a man by the name of Stephens—without any issue. She put the phone on speaker so the receptionist would know she wasn't bluffing. Then she told Detective Stephens who she was and told him she'd gotten his information from Detective Harper.

"I know who you are, Dr. Bryce," Stephens said. "But I knew who you were anyway. Your work for the department through the years makes you something of a celebrity with the NYPD."

Ginny wasn't sure if that was admiration or censure in his voice, but she didn't care. She decided to tell Stephens whatever would bring the quickest response. "Then you know to take seriously what I'm about to say. I discovered that there were three gunmen who attacked us. The third has followed us to the city and is now at Macklin Security. He is threatening Mr. Macklin's life as we speak. Please send help immediately."

"Where are you?" Stephens asked. "Are you safe?"

"I am in the reception area of Macklin Security's building." She rattled off the address, including the floor of the actual office. "If your officers have any trouble finding the elevator, I'm sure the receptionist here will be happy to help. I'm going upstairs."

Even as she said the words, she knew it was a bad idea. She could handle a gun, but she didn't have one on her. She knew how to protect herself in a general sense, and she knew that running toward someone who had tried to kill you wasn't the best way to accomplish that.

"Do not go upstairs!" Stephens bellowed. Without hanging up, he started shouting for officers to assist, peppered with more orders for Ginny to stay where she was. The police were on their way. Ginny ended the call.

Her father's voice rang in her mind, demanding to know if she had any sense at all. She couldn't possibly intend to put her life at risk for a guy she barely knew. She ignored the voice. Though there were a million details about Joseph Macklin she didn't yet know, she trusted him more than anyone she'd ever met. He was a good man, and she would do whatever was necessary to keep him alive so he could get home to Benji.

She met the receptionist's gaze. "If you call upstairs as soon as I get on that elevator and end up alerting the gunman, I'll probably die. And you will be charged for it."

The woman didn't answer, and her face had grown pale and worried. "Shouldn't you wait for the police?"

"Not if it means Mac dies." And with that, Ginny gave up holding herself back and sprinted for the elevator.

21

After the last few days, Mac would have argued that it wasn't possible to surprise him. He probably should have known that couldn't be true. "I don't understand," he said, keeping his voice calm and level. He'd stopped staring at the gun. There was no point. Cal may be office-bound most of the time, but he had been through the same training as Mac and Derrick. The brothers had insisted on it, not wanting their friend to find himself in danger when they weren't around.

Our friend.

"I'm not surprised." Cal stood and circled the desk where he'd been sitting. The younger man perched on the corner of the desk, still pointing the gun at Mac with unwavering aim. "You never did take me seriously."

"Excuse me?" Mac said. "We made you our partner."

Cal laughed, a single harsh bark. "Right, sure. You made me the office boy, and every employee I ever vetted and hired saw it right away. I was the weak friend who couldn't handle anything but computers and accounting, while the golden boys ran the company."

"We welcomed you into our family," Mac said, the shock of the situation beginning to melt into rage. "You were Derrick's best friend since you were both kids."

Cal snorted. "I was the comic relief, the guy everyone thought of as the tagalong."

"That's not true."

"Don't tell me what is and isn't true!" Cal shouted, and as his face reddened, Mac remembered that they weren't having a minor disagreement. Cal was a man with a gun. A man who'd already tried to have him killed.

"Fine," Mac said through gritted teeth. "But I still don't understand how that led to this."

Cal visibly relaxed. He pushed up his glasses with his free hand, a gesture Mac had seen countless times. "It's not as if there weren't advantages to being underrated."

"Oh?" Though still interested in what Cal had to say, Mac was splitting his attention, searching for possible ways out of his current situation. He had to keep Cal talking.

"It let me cut myself a bigger piece of the pie," Cal said.

"You've been embezzling?"

"More than that. I opened my own shadow side of the company. I hired those people you and Derrick deemed too wild, too dangerous. I put them on the kind of lucrative jobs you and your brother wouldn't take because you thought you were the arbiters of morality."

"Hit men?" Mac asked. "You've been hiring them to kill people?"

Cal grinned, and Mac couldn't tell the difference between it and the bright smile the younger man had given him every other time they'd hung out. Cal was excited about sharing his clever plan, and he still wanted Mac to be impressed.

"Some people need killing," Cal answered.

Mac didn't know how to reply to that. The man had been running assassinations using money from Mac and Derrick's company, and they'd never seen it. Never even considered it.

"Don't look so sick," Cal chided. "The jobs didn't always involve killing. Sometimes they were just about intimidation or cleaning up after mistakes. And they paid so well. I've made a fortune."

"And I didn't know about any of it," Mac said. "So why kill me? Do you want so desperately to take over the rest of the business?"

"You're still too stupid for words," Cal said. He shifted position, and Mac saw the first sign of discomfort. Holding a gun on someone for a long time was taxing, and Cal had begun to feel it. Mac couldn't see how to take advantage of that yet, but he hoped it was a good sign.

"Enlighten me," Mac said.

"The problem was that Derrick found a small loose end, something you'd never have noticed, but Derrick was always more of a detail guy than you. I had no idea he'd begun to catch on. Your brother could be so sneaky. He pulled at the thread and followed the trail he found. That's when I realized something had to be done. I couldn't let him reach the end of that trail."

The implications of what Cal was saying hit Mac like a punch in the gut.

Cal wasn't taking advantage of Derrick's death to take over the company—he'd killed Derrick and Madison in the first place.

"You murdered them," Mac growled.

"I sure did," Cal said, his tone almost kind. "Car accidents are far easier to arrange than you'd think."

Mac was shaking from the effort to restrain himself, when all he wanted was to lunge for the other man. But that would merely get him shot. Instead, he had to keep Cal talking until he found a way to take him down. "I had no idea about any of this, so why come after me?"

Cal huffed. "Killing you is a bonus. Once you die, I'll own the company. I mean, I would have gone after you eventually, but you weren't the important target for the gunmen in the woods. The kid was."

"Benji? You wanted to kill a little boy?"

"He was there when his parents died, remember? I followed Derrick and Madison to make sure the accident happened on schedule and the wreck was properly fatal. If not, I would have helped them along. I didn't have to. That car was a mess."

"And Benji saw you," Mac said, realization finally cutting through all the shock.

"He did, but I couldn't get in the car and reach him. I could have shot him, but no one would have thought that was accidental. There would be questions about a gunshot victim in a car accident. People might have started to wonder if maybe it wasn't such an accident. Then I saw how pale he was, so I figured he probably had injuries I couldn't see. Which meant the problem would take care of itself."

Cold horror gripped Mac as he heard the casual way Cal laid out the details of the murder he'd arranged for his best friend and his wife, as well as the attempted murder of his young son. As Mac listened, he realized neither he nor Derrick had ever actually known Cal, not even when he was a kid. They'd thought they did, but the Cal he'd known could not have done something like this.

"You must have been relieved when Benji couldn't talk," Mac managed to say, trying to hide his shock and fury. He couldn't give in and attack Cal directly, not while Cal held the gun on him. He had to survive, because he had no doubt whatsoever that Cal would keep going after Benji.

"Relieved?" Cal said. "I suppose. I thought it would buy me some time. That kind of mutism can take years to break. I read about it. And in that time, Benji might start thinking he imagined seeing me. The mind plays tricks when someone is in shock, after all. And childhood memories aren't always clear."

"Then why send killers after us?"

Cal rolled his eyes. "Because you decided to get the kid some fancy therapist who was known for working miracles with traumatized kids. That's the word the magazine article I read about her used—miracles.

That was one miracle I couldn't allow. You'd be far too quick to believe the kid. I knew that about you."

He stood up then, pointing the gun at Mac with that steady hand again. "So really, this is all your fault. And now, when I'm done with you here, I'll go over and visit Bill. He's a retired cop. The police will think that someone Bill put away during his career came after him, and the kid was collateral damage. Tragic, really."

"That's not going to happen," Mac said. "Not with the attack on me, followed by my murder. How are you going to explain that?"

"There's a clear trail to some rather unsavory characters you and Derrick angered a while back. For an improvisation, it's actually pretty good, if I do say so myself."

"And they killed me in the office, with you here?" Mac asked.

"Yeah, that one could be a problem. Good point. I'll have to leave you here alive and kill you later after I take care of Benji. Then I'll be found shot by the same evil men who came after you. Of course, I'll survive my wounds. That's one miracle I'm okay with."

"Of course," Mac said. "And you think I'll just sit and twiddle my thumbs while you go and kill my nephew."

Cal took another step closer to the desk where Mac still sat. Mac finally saw a glimmer of hope. One more step. If Cal took one more step, Mac could shove the desk at him. He just needed Cal to be knocked off balance for a moment. Mac would have to scale the desk before Cal could shoot him, but he thought it was worth a try.

But Cal didn't take another step forward. He stopped, the gun never wavering, and pulled some plastic flex cuffs from his pocket. He tossed the plastic onto the desk. "Put those on."

"Or what?" Mac couldn't risk being cuffed. He'd still be able to fight, but he didn't intend to agree to anything that made his position worse.

"Or you die right now, and I figure out a new way to explain it."

"The police aren't idiots, Cal. They'll figure this out when I end up dead, especially when I have ligature marks."

Cal snorted. "I can be extremely convincing. Now, put on the cuffs or you're finished."

Mac opened his mouth to say he thought he'd go ahead and die, but the words never came out. He was distracted by a glass baseball hurtling through the air. Mac recognized the baseball. It was part of a trophy he'd won years before. Derrick had insisted the trophy be displayed in a wall-mounted case not far from the door into the office. Mac had never seen the glass baseball airborne.

Cal saw Mac glance behind him, but he never even flinched, probably assuming Mac was trying to distract him. As a result, the glass ball slammed into the back of his head. The pitch was spot on, but though it sent Cal stumbling, it wasn't enough to knock him unconscious or cause him to drop the gun. Instead, Cal stumbled briefly, spun around, and fired off a shot.

It was all the distraction Mac needed. He lunged over the desk and tackled Cal, shoving him to the ground with ease since there was no way the smaller man could take Mac's weight and stay on his feet. Cal tried to squirm and point the gun at Mac, but the gun hadn't been out of Mac's thoughts for a second. He gripped Cal's wrist.

Cal didn't give up easily, and Mac found the smaller man was stronger than he would ever have guessed. Still, he didn't have Mac's bulk, and there was no way he could throw Mac off or control where the gun pointed. It went off again, and Mac heard the bullet lodge in the desk.

Mac slammed Cal's arm against the floor again and again. The plush carpet did its best to absorb the blows, but Mac kept at it.

As they wrestled, the sleeve of Mac's jacket rode up, revealing the bandage on his arm. Cal squirmed again and grabbed the bandage with his free hand. Cal dug his fingers in, making Mac grunt in pain, but he refused to let go of Cal's wrist. No matter what, he couldn't lose control of the gun. But he stopped slamming Cal's arm against the floor and punched Cal in the face instead.

The smaller man gave up, even cringing when Mac raised his hand again. Mac plucked the gun out of Cal's limp hand. He kept it aimed at Cal as he shifted position to grab the flex cuffs Cal had tossed on the desk for him. "These are going to come in handy after all."

Cal glared at him, refusing to take the cuffs.

With a shrug, Mac rolled Cal over and cuffed his wrists behind him. "As it happens," Mac told the man under him, "you're not going to get away with this."

Cal snarled at him.

Mac grinned, and the grin broadened when he heard the sound of sirens. "I think your ride is on the way. Isn't that nice?"

Mac carefully stood, his gaze sweeping the office. The glass baseball hadn't arrived on its own. For an instant, he wondered if Caitlin had followed him up, but he discarded that idea. He could think of only one person who would somehow manage to be there when he needed her most.

"Ginny?" he called.

"I'm here." Ginny's voice was tight, and Mac wondered if she'd found a place to hide after throwing the ball.

"It's all right," he said. "Cal's down."

"Unfortunately," Ginny said, the tightness in her voice taking on a breathless edge, "so am I."

Mac didn't hesitate. He grabbed the gun from the desk, having no intention of leaving it anywhere near Cal, and ran in the direction of Ginny's voice. She was around the arch that connected the office's reception area to the larger office room where the standoff had played out.

Ginny sat, leaning against the wall, her knees drawn up to her chest. She held her hand pressed hard against her shoulder, and blood was soaking through the jacket around her fingers. "I am not as fast as I thought I was."

Mac dropped to his knees. "Let me see."

"I would prefer to keep pressure on the wound," she said. Her voice had grown thinner. "Though if you could find some cloth, I'll pass that job on to you."

Mac stripped off his leather jacket, letting it fall to the office floor as he pulled the silly pony T-shirt over his head.

"Are you sure that's proper office attire?" Ginny asked, and she managed to smile at him.

"I think it's casual Friday," he said as he folded the shirt into a pad, trying to ignore the feelings raging inside him—fear for her and . . . yes, love. "Now let me see that wound."

"It's not Friday," she said, then sucked air sharply through her teeth at the pain as she lifted her hand.

"I never was good at keeping track." Mac pulled her blazer open to better see the entry point. It was still bleeding freely. He pressed the T-shirt firmly to her wound. She hissed again, and he felt terrible. He didn't want to hurt her. He didn't ever want to hurt her.

"I called the cops," she said. "You should put the gun down. They'll get jumpy."

Mac put the gun on the ground well away from him, but his eyes never left her face. "It's going to be okay."

Her face was pale and the pain showed in her eyes, but she still smiled. "I know." The smile grew bigger. "Besides, after the last few days, this is practically a paper cut." Then she tried to laugh with him, but the pain made her moan instead, and she leaned her head against the wall.

Mac opened his mouth to say something encouraging, but the opportunity was lost when the door to the office burst open, and men with drawn guns and bulletproof gear rushed in.

Better late than never.

22

Ginny shuffled across the hardwood floors in her apartment, wondering how long every inch of her body would continue to hurt. Her hospital stay had been short, barely over a day before they pronounced her fine to care for herself as long as she didn't overdo it. The endless stream of police questions once she'd woken up from surgery had made her eager for the quiet of her own home.

She wouldn't have minded all the questions if the police had been willing to answer a few of hers in return, but when she wanted to know about the investigation into Cal, they muttered something about it being ongoing and fired off another question, which often felt like a rewording of something she'd already answered. Finally, the nurses kicked out the police so she could rest. It had been a blessing.

After days stuck in the quiet apartment, she almost wished the police would pop by and let her answer the same questions one more time. Or maybe even drive her down to the station. She'd enjoy some hot lights and bad coffee in exchange for going somewhere and doing something. She might even be able to trick one of them into updating her on the investigation.

She stood in her kitchen and surveyed the area around her. "Why have I never taken up a hobby?" People with hobbies always had something to do, didn't they?

It wasn't that she hadn't tried to work on her book. Getting shot had inspired the publisher to offer her another extension on her deadline, but the ache in her shoulder was enough of a distraction to keep her writing periods short.

Ginny reached for the cabinet where she kept her tea and immediately realized that wasn't a good idea when her shoulder complained. She tried again with her other hand. That was one of the toughest parts—using her nondominant hand for everything.

A rap on the door drew her attention. Since she hadn't heard the buzzer, she knew it had to be Willow. The doorman knew Willow and sent her up immediately whenever she arrived. Ginny headed for the door, grabbing her sling from a hook in the small entryway as she passed it. The doctor had told her to keep her arm in the sling for a few weeks, but Ginny found that far too limiting. Still, she didn't need a lecture about it from Willow. Her assistant had begun to act as if she were Ginny's mother.

Ginny slipped the sling over her neck and then slid her arm in. She tugged the device nice and straight, then began flipping the locks. As she unlocked each one, she made a mental list of tasks for Willow. The list dissolved when the door swung open to reveal Mac and a grinning, bouncing Benji at his side, holding a sheet of paper.

"I tried, but I couldn't keep him away another day," Mac said apologetically. "I know the doctor said you should rest so we won't stay long."

"You two are better medicine than any rest," Ginny said, and meant it. She'd been worried about Mac. Untangling everything Cal had done in the name of the business had to be messy. And that didn't account for the emotional heavy blow of discovering the ultimate betrayal by a longtime family friend and colleague. "Come in."

She stepped back to let them in. Benji eyed her sling, his smile losing a bit of its glow. "It's okay," Ginny said. "I wear this thing because it's stylish. I'm fine."

The doubt on Benji's face couldn't have been clearer.

Ginny bent to speak quietly. "I keep it hanging on that peg right there and only put it on when someone is at the door. My assistant is so bossy about it."

Benji's expression brightened again.

Ginny straightened up. "Is that a picture you're working on?"

Benji glanced at his uncle.

"He wanted to bring it to you," Mac said. "It's a present."

"Wonderful." Ginny held out her good hand and Benji handed her the drawing. She almost expected it to feature the scary man, possibly being chased off by Mac, but the round-eyed horror of Benji's past drawings was gone. So was the obsession with using a black crayon or pencil alone. The drawing featured three figures, all happy and holding hands. One figure was considerably smaller than the other two.

Ginny was delighted by the joy that radiated from the page. "Is this your mom and dad?"

Benji shook his head. He pointed to Mac and then to one of the figures.

"Ah, that's Uncle Mac. It's a very good likeness," Ginny said. She pointed to the second person, slightly smaller than the first. "Is this your uncle Bill?"

Benji giggled and shook his head again. He pointed to Ginny and then to the drawing.

"Oh, forgive me," she said. "I should have recognized my hair." The drawing's hair was a single scribble, but Ginny felt it perfectly captured the struggle to look decent when she wasn't supposed to get her shoulder wet and couldn't lift both hands over her head. "I would love to put this on my fridge so I can see it all the time. Is that okay with you?"

Benji bobbed his head. She noticed him peering curiously around the room. "If you want to explore, feel free. Open drawers or cabinets if you want. I loved doing that when I was a kid. But don't take anything out, okay?"

Benji didn't have to be told twice. He crossed into the living room and peeked behind the cabinet doors of the entertainment center.

Ginny held up the drawing and said to Mac in an undertone, "I don't remember being quite so cheery when we were running through the woods."

"I don't think that drawing is supposed to represent the past," Mac said. "My suspicion is that Benji's hoping for a future trip to the park." He waved a hand toward his nephew. "I assume you don't have anything dangerous he might happen upon?"

"No," Ginny said. "I have a large, locked safe where I keep a handgun, but I doubt Benji can crack a safe yet."

"I'm not sure I'd underestimate him. How are you?"

"In need of escape. Shortly before you arrived, I was thinking about how much I need to get out of this apartment."

"I thought you were supposed to take it easy."

"Walking in the park is easy," Ginny insisted. "I could go with you and Benji. No one will try to attack us there."

Mac chuckled. "On a good day, anyway."

"Want some coffee or tea?" Ginny asked as she headed for the kitchen to hang up Benji's drawing.

"I'd love some, but you have to let me make it," Mac said. "Waiting on people does not qualify as taking it easy."

"You and Willow could start a club of fussy nags," Ginny complained, but she took a seat on one of her counter stools and directed Mac to where she kept the coffee. She was surprised by how comfortable she was with him working in her kitchen, considering her long years of living alone.

When they each had fresh coffee, Ginny dared to ask, "How are you doing?"

"Me?" he asked. "I'm fine. I didn't get shot."

"There are things that are rougher to take than a bullet," she said. "Finding out your brother was murdered by someone you always believed you could trust would be one of those things."

"It hasn't been easy," Mac agreed. "To be honest, one of the hardest parts is the fact that Cal would have gotten away with it if he hadn't been so eager to tie up loose ends. The scale of his operation was incredible. He had actually tracked down the people who did the original work for your father on that cabin. That's how he knew about the tunnel."

"That's dedication," Ginny said. "My dad would have been distraught to have his secrets discovered so easily."

"I suppose I should be grateful to your father," Mac said. "His paranoia saved our lives."

"Don't think I haven't marveled at that," Ginny said. She took a sip of her coffee, enjoying the rich flavor. "How's your business faring?"

"It's going to be rough," Mac said. "The police are still uncovering all the details of Cal's crimes. It's becoming clear he wasn't as clever as he thought he was. He won't get out of this, and neither will the men he hired to do terrible things."

"Good," Ginny said. "That man is a danger to society."

"I can't believe what he used our company for," Mac said. "All Derrick and I ever wanted for Macklin Security was to keep people safe, especially in their most vulnerable times. Having my life's work twisted into something so horrible has been hard to reckon with. Then I feel guilty even thinking about the company in light of finding out that my brother's death was actually murder."

"The heart can grieve more than one thing at a time," Ginny said.

What she didn't say was that she wanted to be the one to help him process his grief. For good.

♡

Mac spun the half-empty coffee mug in his hands, considering his next move. He wanted everything between Ginny and him to be clear and honest, all the time. He'd never met a more honest person in his life. Add to that the fact that she'd literally taken a bullet for him. Theirs was a relationship he didn't want to mess up.

Then leave it alone, a panicky voice inside him commanded. He could do that. He could keep bringing Benji to work with her. His nephew was already much better, but he still had terrible dreams sometimes—not nightly, but often. He was willing to leave Mac's apartment, even eager to take walks or go to the park or do pretty much anything Mac suggested. He sometimes stared off into the distance, but that happened less and less as well.

"How much have you explained to Benji?" Ginny asked, her voice breaking into his thoughts in a surprise that made him jump.

Hopefully the jitters will go away with time. "I told him I know who the scary man was," Mac said. "I told him that man is going to prison and he won't be able to get to Benji ever again. He also knows Cal shot you because you were rescuing me."

"'Rescuing' is an extreme interpretation," she said. "'Improvising' probably comes closer. I was afraid the guy would shoot you before the police arrived."

"I appreciate the assist," Mac said. "But let's not ever do that again."

"Sounds good," she replied. "That bullet ruined my favorite blazer. Well, the bullet along with romping through the woods and crawling into a cave. Regardless, I don't feel like losing any more of my nice clothing."

"I don't think the pony T-shirt survived either," he said, grinning at her. "The hospital never gave it back to me. It's too bad. I loved that shirt."

"I'll keep that in mind," she said. "Maybe you'll get a new one for Christmas."

Mac studied Ginny's open, smiling face. She was so different from the woman he'd seen masterfully capturing the audience as she talked about her work the first time they'd met. That woman had been beautiful too but closed off and distrustful. He liked the present version of Ginny better. She wasn't perfectly made up, and her shirt was buttoned crookedly, though he'd never point it out to her. He realized with a jolt that hers was the face he wanted to gaze at forever.

"There's something I've been wanting to talk to you about," he said.

She'd lifted her mug to her lips again, so she merely raised her eyebrows in question over the rim.

He opened his mouth to say... he wasn't sure what, but probably something incredibly stupid, when a knock sounded at the door.

"That will be Willow," Ginny said, setting down the mug and hopping off the stool. "I thought it was Willow before. How did you get the doorman to let you in without buzzing me?"

Mac followed her to the door. "Benji showed him his drawing. He recognized you in it right away."

She laughed. "He's always been much better at art interpretation than I have."

Ginny opened the door to reveal Willow, who held up a bakery box. "I come bearing gifts," she said, her round face glowing with cheer. "Hey, Mac! I'm so glad you're here. The boss has been a grump from missing you."

"I don't need pastries, especially when I'm not allowed to be active enough to work them off. And I have not missed anyone," Ginny said, but she backed up to let Willow in.

"Sure you haven't," Willow replied with incorrigible brightness. "Now come have some sugar. You need all the sweetening you can get."

"Good to see you, Willow," Mac told her. *But your timing is terrible.*

"Seriously, she's been *such* a grump," Willow said in a stage whisper as she passed by Mac. "Can I hire you to protect me from her?"

Mac laughed.

Benji raced over to join them, screeching to a halt a few feet away to stare up at Willow. Mac had to admit that Ginny's assistant was quite a sight with her abundance of jingling earrings and her vivid pink hair.

The young woman waved the bag at Benji. "You must be Benji. I've heard all about you. I'm Willow. Want a doughnut?"

Benji's face lit up.

"That'll be healthy," Ginny said dryly.

"It's not healthy to eat healthy all the time," Willow insisted, breezing past Benji on her way to the kitchen. "Come on, Benji. I'll get you some milk to have with your doughnut. Milk is healthy. My mom always said so. Glazed or chocolate?"

And to everyone's shock, a quiet little voice answered, "Chocolate, please."

Mac could have fallen through the floor. He felt as if, after months of darkness, the sun was beginning to reach tentative rays over the horizon.

Ginny clutched his arm, her eyes bright with excitement. "Stay calm," she whispered. "We don't want to overreact and startle him back into silence. Though it's taking everything in me not to jump up and down shrieking right now."

Mac knew exactly how she felt.

Fortunately for both of them, Benji's attention was still on Willow, whose demeanor didn't change at all. "Chocolate coming right up, sir. Ginny, if you have to have something healthy, one of these is a blueberry cake doughnut."

"Are you kidding?" Ginny asked, and Mac was impressed that her voice didn't even tremble. "It literally has 'cake' in the name."

"And blueberries. Which are fruit, and therefore healthy," her assistant replied lightly.

Mac heard Ginny sigh beside him. "I've created a monster," she said. "That young woman used to be at least a little intimidated by me. I tell you, they scent weakness, and it's all over."

"I'm not sure 'weak' is a word I'd ever use to describe you," Mac said.

Ginny beamed at him. "Thank you."

Mac and Ginny gazed into each other's eyes for a long moment, and somehow the atmosphere around them changed. It felt charged, as if something new were on the horizon.

"Ginny," Mac said. "I need to tell you something."

"What is it?"

"I want to say first that I want everything between us to be honest. That's why I'm saying this. I'm not trying to put pressure on you."

She frowned in confusion. "Okay."

"Now, you're a psychologist, so you're probably going to say that what I'm feeling is a reaction to everything we've been through, but I want to make it clear right now that isn't the case. What I'm feeling is a reaction to getting to know you, to seeing that you're a lot more than a brilliant, intimidating woman, though you are both of those things."

Her expression changed to one of exaggerated patience, but she didn't interrupt him. She merely continued to study his face.

"You're also caring and brave—the bravest person I've ever met. You can also be infuriating and stubborn, but I find I enjoy those things about you too. In fact, I love them."

"You do?" She asked the question lightly, and he could see the faintest trace of amusement in her eyes.

"Are you laughing at me?" he asked.

"No," she said. "I'm simply glad you're the one who got to make the incredibly awkward declaration, because I suspect I would have sounded every bit as bad, and I prefer to maintain as much dignity as I can."

"That sounds like an insult. I think."

"Nope. It's a way to say that I feel the same way, Mac. You're bossy, sure of yourself, and entirely too handsome, but you were born to be a hero. And I love you."

He gaped openly at the simple statement. "You do?"

With her good hand, she grabbed a fistful of his shirt and pulled him down toward her face. "I do." Then she kissed him, and fireworks roared through his whole body.

When she finally released him and he remembered how to speak, it was the truth that came out. "I love you too, Ginny."